blubber

Books by Judy Blume

YOUNG ADULT AND MIDDLE GRADE

Are You There God? It's Me, Margaret.

Deenie

Forever . . .

Here's to You, Rachel Robinson

Iggie's House

It's Not the End of the World

Just as Long as We're Together

Letters to Judy: What Kids Wish They Could Tell You

Places I Never Meant to Be: Original Stories by Censored Writers
(edited by Judy Blume)

Starring Sally J. Freedman as Herself

Then Again, Maybe I Won't

Tiger Eyes

THE FUDGE BOOKS

Tales of a Fourth Grade Nothing

Otherwise Known as Sheila the Great

Superfudge

Fudge-a-mania

Double Fudge

PICTURE BOOKS AND STORYBOOKS

The Pain and the Great One

The One in the Middle Is the Green Kangaroo

Freckle Juice

The Pain and the Great One series

Soupy Saturdays

Cool Zone

Going, Going, Gone!

Friend or Fiend?

JUDY BLUME

blubber

A Richard Jackson Book
Atheneum Books for Young Readers
New York London Toronto
Sydney New Delhi

ATHENEUM BOOKS FOR YOUNG READERS

An imprint of Simon & Schuster Children's Publishing Division
1230 Avenue of the Americas, New York, New York 10020

Cover design by Lauren Rille, interior design by Tom Daly
The text for this book was set in New Century Schoolbook LT Std.
Manufactured in the United States of America
0718 OFF
This Atheneum Books for Young Readers paperback proprietary edition June 2016
2 4 6 8 10 9 7 5 3
ISBN 978-1-4814-8981-2 (proprietary paperback edition)

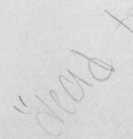

For Randy and Larry,
my experts on fifth grade, loose teeth,
The Guinness Book of World Records,
stamp collecting and school bus action

blubber

1

"It's very foolish to laugh if you don't know what's funny in the first place."

My best friend, Tracy Wu, says I'm really tough on people. She says she wonders sometimes how I can like her. But we both know that's a big joke. Tracy's the best friend I'll ever have. I just wish we were in the same fifth-grade class.

My teacher is Mrs. Minish. I'm not crazy about her. She hardly ever opens the windows in our room because she's afraid of getting a stiff neck. I never heard anything so dumb. Somedays our room gets hot and stuffy and it smells—like this afternoon. We'd been listening to individual reports on The Mammal for almost an hour. Donna Davidson was standing at the front of the room reading hers. It was on the horse. Donna has this *thing* about horses.

I tried hard not to fall asleep but it wasn't easy. For a while I watched Michael and Irwin as they passed a *National Geographic* back and forth. It was open to a page full of naked people. Wendy and Caroline played Tic Tac Toe behind Wendy's notebook. Wendy won three games in a row. I wasn't surprised. Wendy is a very clever person. Besides being class president, she is also group science leader, recess captain and head of the goldfish committee.

Did Mrs. Minish notice anything that was going on or was she just concentrating on Donna's boring report? I couldn't tell from looking at her. She had a kind of half-smile on her face and sometimes she kept her eyes closed for longer than a blink.

To make the time go faster I thought about Halloween. It's just two days away. I love to dress up and go Trick-or-Treating, but I'm definitely not going to be a dumb old witch again this year. Donna will probably be a horse. She dresses up like one every Halloween. Last year she said when she grows up she is going to marry a horse. She has him all picked out and everything. His name is San Salvador. Most of the time Donna smells like a horse but I wouldn't tell her that because she might think it's a compliment.

I yawned and wiggled around in my chair.

"In closing," Donna said, "I would like you to remember that even though some people say horses are stupid that is a big lie! I personally happen to know some very smart horses. And that's the end of my report."

The whole class clapped, not because Donna's report was great, but because it was finally over. Mrs. Minish opened her eyes and said, "Very nice, Donna."

Earlier, when I had finished my report on the lion, Mrs. Minish said the same thing to me. *Very nice, Jill.* Just like that. Now I couldn't be sure if she really meant it. My report wasn't as dull as Donna's but it wasn't as long either. Maybe the longer you talk the better grade you get. That wouldn't be fair though. Either way, I'm glad Mrs. Minish calls on us alphabetically and that my last name is Brenner. I come right after Bruce Bonaventura.

Mrs. Minish cleared her throat. "Linda Fischer will give the last report for today," she said. "We'll hear five more tomorrow and by the middle of next week everyone will have had a turn."

I didn't think I'd be able to live through another report.

"Are you ready, Linda?" Mrs. Minish asked.

"Yes," Linda said, as she walked to the front of the room. "My report is uh . . . on the whale."

Caroline and Wendy started another game of Tic Tac Toe while Bruce went to work on his nose. He has a very interesting way of picking it. First he works one nostril and then the other and whatever he gets out he sticks on a piece of yellow paper inside his desk.

The hand on the wall clock jumped. Only ten minutes till the bell. I took a piece of paper out of my desk to keep a record of how many times Linda said *And uh* . . . while she gave her report. So far I'd counted seven.

4

Linda's head is shaped like a potato and sits right on her shoulders, as if she hasn't got any neck. She's also the pudgiest girl in our class, but not in our grade. Ruthellen Stark and Elizabeth Ryan are about ten times fatter than Linda, but even they can't compare to Bruce. If we had a school fat contest he would definitely win. He's a regular butterball.

"Blubber is a thick layer of fat that lies under the skin and over the muscles of whales," Linda said. "And uh . . . it protects them and keeps them warm even in cold water. Blubber is very important. Removing the blubber from a whale is a job done by men called flensers. They peel off the blubber with long knives and uh . . . cut it into strips." Linda held up a picture. "This is what blubber looks like," she said.

Wendy passed a note to Caroline. Caroline read it, then turned around in her seat and passed it to me. I unfolded it. It said: *Blubber is a good name for her!* I smiled, not because I thought the note was funny, but because Wendy was watching me. When she turned away I crumpled it up and left it in the corner of my desk. The next thing I knew, Robby Winters, who sits next to me, reached out and grabbed it.

Linda kept talking. "And uh . . . whale oil is obtained by heating the blubber of the whale. European margarine companies are the chief users of whale oil and uh . . . it also goes into glycerine and some laundry soaps and has other minor uses. Sometimes Eskimos and Japanese eat blubber . . ."

When Linda said that Wendy laughed out loud and once she started she couldn't stop. Probably the reason she got the hiccups was she laughed too hard. They were very loud hiccups. The kind you can't do anything about.

Pretty soon Robby Winters was laughing too. He doesn't laugh like an ordinary person— that is, no noise comes out. But his whole body shakes and tears run out of his eyes and just watching him is enough to make anybody start in, so the next minute we were all roaring—all except Linda and Mrs. Minish. She clapped her hands and said, "Exactly what is going on here?"

Wendy let out a loud hiccup.

Mrs. Minish said, "Wendy, you are excused. Go and get a drink of water."

Wendy stood up and ran out of the room.

By then Wendy's note about Blubber had travelled halfway around the class and I couldn't stop laughing, even when Mrs. Minish looked right at me and said, "Jill Brenner, will you please explain the joke."

I didn't say anything.

"Well, Jill . . . I'm waiting . . ."

"I don't know the joke," I finally said, finding it hard to talk at all.

"You don't know why you're laughing?" Mrs. Minish asked.

I shook my head.

"It's very foolish to laugh if you don't know what's funny in the first place."

I nodded.

"If you can't control yourself you can march straight to Mr. Nichols' office and explain the situation to him."

I nodded again.

"I'm waiting for your answer, Jill."

"I forgot the question, Mrs. Minish."

"The question is, can you control yourself?"

"Oh . . . yes, Mrs. Minish . . . I can."

"I hope so. Linda, you may continue," Mrs. Minish said.

"I'm done," Linda told her.

"Well . . . that was a very nice report."

The bell rang then. We pushed back our chairs and ran for the row of lockers behind our desks. Mrs. Minish has to dismiss us at exactly two thirty-five. Otherwise we'd miss our buses.

It's very important to get on the right one. On the first day of school my brother, Kenny, got on the wrong bus and wound up all the way across town. Since my mother and father were both at work the principal of Longmeadow School had to drive Kenny home. I would never make such a mistake. My bus is H-4. That means Hillside School, route number four. I'm glad Kenny doesn't go to my school. Next year he will, but right now he is just in fourth grade and only fifth and sixth graders go to Hillside.

When I got on the bus Tracy was saving me a seat. Caroline and Wendy found two seats across from us. Before this year I'd never been in either one of their classes but this is my second time with Linda Fischer and I've been with Donna, Bruce and Robby since kindergarten.

"We had the best afternoon," Tracy said. "Mr. Vandenburg invented this game to help us get our multiplication facts straight and I was *forty-eight* and every time he called out *six times eight* or *four times twelve* I had to jump up and yell *Here!* It was so much fun."

"You're lucky to be in his class," I said. "I wish he'd give Mrs. Minish some ideas."

"She's the wrong type."

"You're telling me!"

As Linda climbed onto the bus Wendy shouted, "Here comes Blubber!" And a bunch of kids called out, "Hi, Blubber."

Our bus pulled out of the driveway and as soon as we turned the corner and got going Robby Winters sailed a paper airplane down the aisle. It landed on my head.

"Pass it here, Jill," Wendy called. When I

did, she whipped out a Magic Marker and wrote *I'm Blubber—Fly Me* on the wing. Then she stood up and aimed the plane at Linda.

The group of girls who always sit in the last row of seats started singing to the tune of "Beautiful Dreamer," *Blubbery blubber . . . blub, blub, blub, blub . . .*

At the same time, the airplane landed on two sixth-grade boys who ripped it up to make spit balls. They shot them at Linda. Then Irwin grabbed her jacket off her lap. "She won't need a coat this winter," he said. "She's got her blubber to keep her warm." He tossed the jacket up front and we played Keep-Away with it.

"Some people even eat blubber!" Caroline shrieked, catching Linda's jacket. "She said so herself."

"Ohhh . . . disgusting!" Ruthellen Stark moaned, clutching her stomach.

"Sick!"

The girls in the back started their song again. *Blubbery blubber . . . blub, blub, blub, blub . . .*

The bus driver yelled, "Shut up or I'll put you all off!"

Nobody paid any attention.

Linda picked the spit balls out of her hair but she still didn't say anything. She just sat there, looking out the window.

When we reached the first stop Wendy threw Linda's jacket to me. She and Caroline ran down the aisle and as Linda stood up, Wendy called back, "Bye, Blubber!"

Linda stopped at my row. I could tell she was close to crying because last year, when Robby stepped on her finger by mistake, she got the same look on her face, right before the tears started rolling.

"Oh, here," I said and I tossed her the jacket. She got off and I saw her race down the street away from Wendy and Caroline. They were still laughing.

2

"That's what you're going to be for Halloween?"

Linda lives in Hidden Valley. So do Wendy, Caroline, Robby and a bunch of other kids. It's a big group of houses with a low brick wall around it and a sign that says WELCOME TO HIDDEN VALLEY—SPEED LIMIT 25 MILES PER HOUR. Across the street there is another sign saying WATCH OUR CHILDREN. It's called Hidden Valley because there are a million trees and in the summer you can't see any of the houses. Nobody told me this. It's something I figured out by myself.

My stop is next. Me and Tracy are the only ones who get off there. The Wu family lives across the road from us. They have a lot of animals. All of this doesn't mean we live in the country. It's kind of pretend country. That is, it looks like country because of all the woods but just about everyone who lives here works in the city, like my mother and father. I don't know one single farmer unless you count the woman who sells us vegetables in the summer.

"Can you come over?" Tracy asked, as we collected the mail from our mailboxes.

"As soon as I change," I told her.

"Bring your stamps," Tracy said.

"I will." Me and Tracy are practically professional stamp collectors. We both have the *Master Global Album.* And I have this deal going with my father—if I let my nails grow between now and Christmas he will give me $25 to spend in Gimbels, which has the best stamp department in the whole world. So even though it is just about killing me, I'm not going to bite my nails. Sometimes I have to sit on my fingers to keep from doing it.

When I got home Kenny was waiting at the front door. He was holding his *Guinness Book of World Records* in one hand and with the other was shoving a cupcake into his mouth. "Did you know the oldest woman to ever give birth to a baby was fifty-seven years old?" As he talked he blew crumbs out of his mouth.

"So?" I said, to show I wasn't interested, because if Kenny gets the idea I'm interested he will tell me facts from his *Book of World Records* all day.

"So . . . that means Grandma is too old to have a baby."

"Well, of course she is! She's past sixty."

"And Mrs. Sandmeier's too old, too."

Mrs. Sandmeier is our housekeeper. She takes care of me and Kenny after school.

"Too old for what?" she asked, as we walked into the kitchen.

"Too old to have a baby," Kenny said.

Mrs. Sandmeier laughed. "Who says so?"

"My *Book of World Records*," Kenny told her. "The oldest woman to give birth was fifty-seven and you're fifty-eight."

"Don't remind me!" Mrs. Sandmeier said.

Mrs. Sandmeier is always telling us she's

getting old but she can still take on Kenny and his friends at basketball and beat them single-handed.

"How was your day, Jill?" Mrs. Sandmeier asked me in French, as she poured a glass of milk.

I answered in English. "Pretty good."

Mrs. Sandmeier made a face. Part of her job is to teach me and Kenny to speak French. She's from Switzerland and can speak three languages. I understand what she says when she speaks French but I always answer in English because most of the time I'm too busy to think of the right words in French.

After my snack, I changed into my favorite jeans, collected my stamp equipment, and headed for Tracy's. Kenny and Mrs. Sandmeier were already outside, practicing lay-ups.

"Be back at five-thirty," Mrs. Sandmeier called, as I walked up the driveway.

"I will."

Our street isn't big enough to have a name. There's just a sign saying PRIVATE ROAD, and our house and Tracy's. Dr. Wu was outside planting tulip bulbs. Tuesday is his day off.

"Hi, Dr. Wu," I said. He is our family doctor and makes house calls only to us. I like him a lot. He's always smiling. Also, he doesn't gag me with a stick when he looks down my throat.

"Hi, yourself," he called to me.

Tracy was in the backyard, feeding her chickens. She has ten of them and a beautiful white rooster called Friendly, who I love. Sometimes Tracy lets me hold him. His crown is red and it feels like a cat's tongue. I know this because last year one of Tracy's cats licked me. She has seven cats but they don't live in the house. They come into the garage to get food and water and the rest of the time they stay outside. Tracy also has two dogs. They live in the house.

When the chickens were fed we went inside to Tracy's room to look over our latest approvals from the Winthrop Stamp Company. We decided we'd each buy two stamps.

Tracy showed me the Halloween costume her mother is making for her—Big Bird from

Sesame Street. It has yellow feathers and everything.

"It's beautiful!" I said. I still didn't have an idea for my costume.

We went to work on our albums, trading doubles and fastening loose stamps to the page. And then, right in the middle of licking a stamp hinge, I thought up a costume so clever I didn't even tell Tracy. I decided it would be a surprise.

That night, when my mother and father got home, they brought two big pumpkins with them.

I waited until we were halfway through with dinner before I brought up the subject of my Halloween costume. "I don't think I want to be a witch this year," I said. I hoped I wouldn't hurt Mom's feelings because the witch's costume was hers when she was a kid. It has funny, pointy-toed shoes with silver buckles, a high black silk hat and a long black robe with a bow at the neck. The whole thing smells like mothballs. Besides, the shoes hurt my feet.

"You can be whatever you want," my mother said and she didn't sound insulted.

"If she doesn't want to wear the witch's suit, can I?" Kenny asked.

"A boy witch?" I said.

"Sure. What's wrong with that?"

"Nothing," Mom told him. "I'd love to have you wear my costume."

"And I'm going to carry a broom," Kenny said. "And remember that fake cigar from my last year's disguise . . . I'm going to use that too. I'll bet there aren't many witches around who smoke cigars."

"Smoking is dangerous to your health!" I said.

"My cigar's fake, stupid!"

I gave him a kick under the table and was pleased to see that Mom ground out the ciga-rette she'd been smoking.

"What about you, Jill?" my father asked. "What do you want to be?"

"Oh . . . I've been thinking I might like to be a flenser."

"What's that?" Kenny asked.

"You mean you don't know?" I said.

"Never heard of it."

"With all your facts in the *Book of World Records* you never learned about the oldest flenser and the youngest flenser and the flenser who did the best job and all that?"

"Dad . . ." Kenny said. "She's starting in again."

I absolutely love to tease Kenny.

"Jill, that's enough," my father said. "Tell Kenny what a flenser is."

"Yes," Mom said. "I can hardly wait to hear myself."

"You mean you don't know either?" I asked my mother.

"Never heard the word. Did you, Gordon?"

"Nope," Dad said.

Kenny jumped up. "I'll be right back," he told us, as he ran out of the room.

I knew where he was going—to look up "flenser" in his dictionary.

In a few minutes he was back, carrying it. "A flenser strips the blubber off whales," he read, looking at me. "That's what you're going to be for Halloween?" he asked, like he couldn't believe it.

I smiled.

"Where did you get that idea, Jill?" Mom asked.

"From this girl in my class. She gave a report on whales."

"Well . . . that's certainly original," Dad said.

"What kind of costume does a flenser wear?" Kenny asked.

"A flenser suit," I told him.

"Yeah . . . but what's it made of?"

"Oh . . . jeans and a shirt and a special kind of hat and a long knife."

"No knife," my father said. "That's too dangerous."

"Not a *real* knife," I said. "One made out of cardboard."

"What kind of hat?" Kenny asked.

"A flenser hat, naturally," I told him.

"Yeah . . . but what's it look like?"

"I can't begin to describe it. You'll just have to wait and see."

"I'd wear boots if I was a flenser," Kenny said.

"What for?" I asked him.

"Because of walking around in all that yucky blubber stuff."

Kenny was right. I'd have to wear boots too.

After dinner we went into the living room for our family poker game. I handed out the Monopoly money. We each get $150 from the bank. My father shuffled the cards, Mom cut them and Kenny dealt.

I got a pair of kings and three junk cards. I'm careful not to give my hand away by the expression on my face. You can always tell what Kenny is holding. If it's something good he makes all kinds of noises and he laughs a lot. Even if he doesn't have anything good he stays in and takes three new cards. He never drops out when he should because he can't stand not betting against the rest of us.

When it comes to bluffing my father is the best. Every time he stays in and starts raising I think he has three aces and unless I have something really great I drop out. Then I'll find out Dad didn't even have a pair. My mother is not an experienced poker player. She can never remember which is higher—a flush or a straight. Sometimes I have to help her out.

Later, when me and Kenny were in our pajamas and ready for bed, my father said we could carve our pumpkins. Mom had to go to her room because the smell of pumpkin guts makes her sick to her stomach.

Last year, when I cut out my pumpkin's face, it was all lopsided, but this time I got both eyes even and the nose in between. Dad made the teeth for me. Kenny wouldn't let anyone touch his pumpkin, which is why it turned out looking like it had three eyes and no teeth.

3

"And now . . . for the most original
costume of the day . . ."

The next night I turned my mother's old beach
hat into part of my flenser suit. Mom didn't
mind because she'd worn the hat for four
years and was getting tired of it. My mother
never sets foot on the beach without wearing
a floppy hat. She thinks it's very bad to get
sun on her face. She's always saying that sun
makes wrinkles and wrinkles make people
look older and that someday I will know what
she means. My father doesn't worry about
wrinkles so he never has to wear anything on
his head. I'll be like him when I grow up. How
can you dive under the waves with a floppy
hat on your head?

I look much older in the beach hat. I could pass for twelve, I think, maybe even thirteen with sun glasses. The beach hat is so big it covers most of my face. It used to be lots of different colors but now it's faded into a kind of bluish-gray.

I tried to find pictures of whales to decorate the hat but I couldn't so I settled for some of dolphins instead. I cut them out and stapled them all over the brim. Then I cut a piece of black construction paper into thin strips and attached them too. They hung down the sides, kind of like hair.

I shaped my flenser knife like a sword, but with a big curl at one end. I covered it with gold sparkle and painted my boots to match. Then I tried on my whole costume.

I went to my mother's room to have a look in her long mirror but Kenny was already there, admiring himself in the witch's suit. He had on his yellow goggles and the fake cigar dangled out of the corner of his mouth. He was doing some strange dance but as soon as he saw me he stopped.

"I just wanted to see if it fit okay," he said. He walked away from the mirror, tripping over the pointy witch's shoes. "It's hard to walk in these things," he told me, kicking them off.

"Can I ask you a very simple question?" I said.

"Go ahead . . ."

"Why are you wearing your goggles?"

"If you have to ask you wouldn't understand," Kenny told me. "But speaking of goggles . . . did you know that the first motorcycle race was in France, in 1897?"

"No, I didn't. But thanks for telling me."

Kenny looked me up and down. "Is that what you're wearing tomorrow?"

"Yes, it's my flenser suit." I stood in front of the mirror and held the sword out.

"What'd you do to your boots?"

"Painted them."

"Gold?"

"Why not . . ."

"Does Mom know?"

"They're *my* boots, Kenny. Why should

Mom care if I had to paint them to match my sword?"

"Speaking of swords . . ." Kenny began.

"We were *not* speaking of swords," I told him. "We were speaking about my flenser suit!"

"Yeah . . . well, if I were you I'd wear a sign telling people what you are . . . because I don't think anybody's going to know otherwise."

"Oh Kenny . . . you are *so* dumb! Of course they'll know. Just look at my hat . . . can't you see all the pictures of whales up there?"

"They're dolphins," Kenny said.

"Only *you* would know that!"

"And speaking of dolphins," Kenny said.

"Never mind . . . never mind! I don't want to hear it."

Later, I made a sign saying *FLENSER*, just in case Kenny was right. I punched two holes through it, ran a string across and hung it around my neck.

The next morning my mother was surprised when she saw my boots. "They're gold!" Mom said in a very loud voice. She puffed hard on her cigarette.

"Smoking causes cancer and heart disease," I told her, ignoring my boots.

Mom mashed her cigarette out and reached for her coffee. "What did you do to your new boots, Jill?"

"I painted them."

"Jill . . . they have to last you all winter. You haven't even worn them yet."

"I know it, Mother!"

"Well . . . how could you do such a thing?"

"A flenser wouldn't wear plain brown boots."

"I just hope you used washable paint."

"I think I did."

"You checked first, didn't you?"

"I'm almost sure it's washable."

"You didn't check before you used it?"

"Not exactly."

Mom lit another cigarette.

I called for Tracy. She was in her Big Bird costume and her mother was adjusting a crown of feathers on her head. "How do you like it?" she asked, twirling around.

"Oh, Tracy . . . you look fantastic!" Next to her I felt very plain.

Tracy looked me over. "What's a flenser?" she asked, reading my sign.

"That's what I'm supposed to be," I told her.

"I know . . . but what is one?"

"Oh . . . a flenser's a guy who strips the blubber off whales."

"Where'd you get such a weird idea?" Tracy asked.

"From Linda Fischer . . . you know . . . the one Wendy calls Blubber. She gave a report on whales."

"Well," Tracy said, "at least you don't have to worry that everyone will be dressed like you." She went to the mirror and combed her hair. She has the nicest hair I've ever seen. It hangs straight down her back. She can even sit on it. And it never looks dirty or has tangles. I'm growing mine but no matter how long it gets it will never look like Tracy's.

Mrs. Wu drove us to school so Tracy wouldn't

mess up her costume. When I got to my class Wendy was already there. She was dressed like a queen. She wore a very high crown with lots of fake emeralds and rubies pasted to it. She also wore her mother's long bathrobe and had this crazy looking fur thing wrapped around her neck. It had eyes, paws, a tail and everything.

"Animals are for loving, not wearing," I told her.

"I know it," Wendy said, "but this thing is very old. It belonged to my grandmother. And in those days they didn't know about ecology."

"Oh . . ." I said. "Then I guess it's all right."

Donna Davidson really fooled me. Instead of dressing up like a horse, this year she was a jockey. "My things are all *genuine*," she bragged. "My father knows this jockey who's very famous and he's just my size and these are his *real life* jockey clothes."

Donna looked pretty good, but I didn't tell her I thought so. And I wasn't worried about winning the prize for most original costume because a flenser is a lot more clever than a jockey or a queen with a tall crown. Practically everyone else in our class was dressed like a bum, with old baggy pants and shirts hanging out and charcoal smudges on their faces. Caroline even carried a stick with a pouch tied on one end. There is nothing very original about dressing up like that.

Right after Mrs. Minish took the attendance she told us to line up for the Halloween assembly. "Remember, no talking in the halls or the auditorium."

I stood on line between Wendy and Linda, who was wearing a long, red cape. As we walked down the hall Linda tapped me and said, "What are you supposed to be?"

"Can't you read?" I asked, holding up my sign.

"Oh . . . a flenser. I'll bet you got that idea from my report."

"What makes you think so?"

"Jill Brenner!" Mrs. Minish snapped. "I said *no* talking!"

In the auditorium our class sat in the third

and fourth rows. I whispered to Linda, "What are *you* supposed to be?"

"Never mind."

"Don't you know?"

"I know."

"Then tell me."

"No . . . it's my own business."

"I'll bet you're supposed to be Little Red Riding Hood."

"I am not."

I turned to Wendy. "Get a load of Little Red Riding Hood," I said.

Wendy leaned across me and told Linda, "You better watch out for the Big Bad Wolf!"

"Yeah . . ." I said, "you better . . ." I felt a hand on my head. I turned around in my seat. It was Mrs. Minish.

"If I have to speak to you again you'll go back to the classroom."

I didn't say a word during the Pledge of Allegiance or "The Star-Spangled Banner." Linda sang in a very loud voice and when I looked at her I could see her gray tooth. Wendy says if she isn't more careful about the way she brushes all her teeth will turn gray and rotten and fall out.

The Halloween Parade was next. Every class had a turn to march across the stage. The costume judges all sat in the first row. They were mothers from the P.-T.A. It's against the rules for them to vote for their own kids.

I watched carefully as the other classes had their turns. I pretended to be a judge. Only two sixth-graders were dressed as anything besides bums. Jerry Pochuk was a doctor and Fred Yarmouth was something I couldn't figure out. I certainly didn't see any costumes as original as mine or any that were prettier than Tracy's.

After the parade Mrs. Runyon, the librarian, stood on the stage and said, "I'm happy to be here today to present the prizes for the most beautiful and the most original costumes."

I sat on my hands to keep from chewing my nails.

"But before I do, I want to share with you the fine prizes the P.-T.A. has selected and donated." Mrs. Runyon held up two paperback books. They both had medals printed on the covers. I read them last year. One wasn't too bad but the other was so boring I never got past the first chapter. Still, it wasn't the prize that mattered. It was the idea of winning.

"And now . . . for our winner . . ." Mrs. Runyon said. "For the most beautiful costume . . . Tracy Wu, the Big Bird!"

Everyone clapped as Tracy ran to the stage, dripping yellow feathers all over the aisle. She got the boring book.

"And now . . . for the most original costume of the day . . ."

I sat up in my seat.

"To Fred Yarmouth, the fried *egg*," Mrs. Runyon called.

I couldn't believe it! I was so sure the prize would be mine. And how did the judges know Fred was supposed to be a fried egg when I had no idea what he was?

Fred ran to the stage. Mrs. Runyon said, "Tell us, Fred, how did you decide to be a fried egg?"

"Oh, I don't know," Fred said. "I had this

white sheet and some yellow felt and when I put it all together that's what it looked like to me."

He hadn't even planned to be an egg. That made everything worse. Now I'd be stuck wearing gold boots for the rest of the year—and all for nothing.

4

"What's the magic word?"

We were back in our classroom at ten-thirty and Mrs. Minish said we'd work on math and science until lunchtime. I tried to concentrate on my math but when Mrs. Minish asked to see my paper she drew red lines across every problem.

"They're all wrong?" I asked.

"Not the answers," Mrs. Minish said.

"Then what?"

"You didn't set up the problems properly."

"But if I got the right answers what's the difference?"

"Your equations are backwards. You'll have to do the paper over."

"I don't see why," I told her.

"Because you're supposed to be learning how to think the problems through and you aren't thinking the right way."

"Isn't there more than one way to think?"

"Really Jill . . . I don't care for this talking back!"

"But Mrs. Minish . . ."

"No buts," Mrs. Minish said. "Take it home and do it over."

Before lunch Mrs. Minish excused us to go to the Girls' and Boys' Rooms. I took my sword with me. I was afraid if I left it at my desk Robby Winters might get his hands on it and ruin it. And I needed it for later, to go Trick-or-Treating for Unicef.

"Mrs. Minish is such a bitch!" I said to Wendy and Caroline, as we stood by the sinks in the Girls' Room. "She marked all my math problems wrong."

"I got a hundred," Caroline said.

"That's because I let you copy off me," Wendy told her.

"Not that my morning wasn't already

ruined," I said. "I still can't believe they gave that smelly fried-egg costume the prize."

"Yeah," Wendy said. "My costume was much more original than that."

Caroline said, "Personally, I thought Donna Davidson would win. Her things were all genuine."

"There's nothing original about being a jockey," I said. "Being a flenser is original but those judges were too dumb to know it."

"One of them was my aunt," Caroline said.

"Oh . . . I didn't mean to insult her."

"That's all right. She is dumb. My mother's always saying so."

"Oh."

The other girls finished and went back to the classroom while me, Caroline and Wendy stood around talking.

I heard a toilet flush, then Linda Fischer came out of a booth, pulling her red cape around her.

"Look who's here," Wendy said. "It's Blubber!"

"In the flesh," Caroline added.

"I wonder what's under her cape?" Wendy asked.

"Probably nothing," Caroline said.

"Oh, there's got to be something," Wendy said. "There's got to be her blubber . . . at least."

"Yeah . . . her blubber's under her cape!" Caroline said and she and Wendy started laughing. I giggled a little too.

Wendy moved closer to Linda, humming "Beautiful Dreamer."

"Stay away from me!" Linda told her, walking backwards.

"I'm not going to hurt you, stupid," Wendy said. "I just want to see what's under your cape."

"Don't touch me!"

"Oh, don't worry . . . that's not my job . . . Jill's the flenser."

"That's true," I said. "I am."

"And the flenser's the one who strips the blubber," Wendy said.

I wasn't sure exactly what Wendy had in mind.

Linda tried to run but Caroline and Wendy blocked her way.

"Strip her, flenser!" Wendy called. "Now! Then we'll throw her cape out the window and she'll have to walk down the hall in her blubbery birthday suit."

"No!" Linda said. "Don't you dare strip me!"

Caroline and Wendy grabbed hold of Linda's arms and held her still.

"Do your job," Wendy said. "Prove what a good flenser you are."

"Okay," I said, pulling off Linda's cape. She had on a regular skirt and shirt under it.

"Strip her some more!" Wendy said, yanking up Linda's skirt. "Hey . . . Blubber wears flowered underpants."

"Let go of me!" Linda squirmed and tried to kick but Caroline grabbed her shirt and tugged until two buttons popped off.

"She wears an undershirt!" Caroline said.

Linda started to cry.

"Oh my . . . Blubber's blubbering," Wendy said.

"Stop it . . . stop it!" Linda cried.

"What's the magic word?" I asked.

"Please!" Linda's nose was running.

"Blubber knows the magic word," I said, "so the flenser won't strip her today."

"But she still has to obey the queen," Wendy said. "I am Her Majesty, Queen Wendy. Get it, Blubber?"

Linda nodded and tried to catch her breath. She had red splotches all over her face.

"Curtsy to the queen," Wendy said.

Linda tried to tuck her shirt back into her skirt.

"Didn't you hear me, Blubber? I said, curtsy to the queen."

Linda curtsied to Wendy.

"That's better," Wendy said. "Now kiss my foot."

"I don't want to." Linda started sniffling.

I raised my sword. "Do whatever Queen Wendy says, Blubber."

Linda bent down and kissed Wendy's sneaker.

"Now, cut out that stupid crying," Wendy told her, as she threw Linda her cape.

"Here . . . put this on . . . and remember . . . one word to anyone about this and we'll *really* get you next time." Wendy looked at me and smiled.

I wasn't worried about Linda telling on us. Besides, everybody knows you don't cross Wendy.

5

"A person gets what she deserves."

"I won the prize for most original costume in my school," Kenny said. He was still in his witch's suit, standing at the front door, when I got home.

"I don't believe you."

Kenny held up an envelope. "See for yourself." He handed it to me.

I opened the envelope and pulled out a piece of stiff red paper. It said, *One Free Meal at Opie's/Awarded by the P.-T.A. of Longmeadow School for the Most Original Halloween Costume.* Under that, *Kenny Brenner* was printed in blue ink.

"You see?" Kenny said. "I told you I won."

"Opie's has rat tails in their food."

"Just in the chicken," Kenny said. "The hamburgers are okay."

"I wouldn't eat there if it was the last place on earth!"

"You don't have to," Kenny said.

"At my school they at least gave away paperback books."

"Did you get one?"

"I already read them both," I told him.

"But did you get one?"

"They gave it to Fred Yarmouth, just because he's in sixth grade."

Kenny smiled and went tripping down the hall to his room.

I kicked the front door shut and went to the kitchen. "I don't understand it," I told Mrs. Sandmeier. "I wore that witch's suit three years in a row and I never won anything."

Mrs. Sandmeier offered me a plate of gingersnaps. "It was the cigar that did it," she said. "That and the yellow goggles. He was an unusual witch."

"Next year he'll probably be an unusual flenser and win again."

"Probably," Mrs. Sandmeier said.

"Hmph!" I took three gingersnaps and went to my room. I opened my closet and took out my special suitcase. I keep my stamp collection in it. Grandma gave me the suitcase last year, before she moved to her apartment. She kept it in her basement for fifteen years, ever since Grandpa died. All that time she was just waiting to find someone who would really appreciate it. She chose me because she knew I would take good care of it, and I do. I polish it with a special leather cream once a week.

I turned the pages of my *Master Global Album*, admiring all my stamps. The ones from Nagaland are my favorites.

Tracy called at five. "What time will you be ready to go Trick-or-Treating?"

I swallowed the meatball I'd been chewing and said, "As soon as my parents get home. I'm eating now."

"Don't forget your pillowcase."

"I won't. I cut out eyes and everything."

"Good . . . because if Mr. Machinist takes pictures this year I don't want him getting me."

"Me neither."

"I'll meet you outside at six-thirty."

"Okay . . ."

"And bring a flashlight."

"Right."

"Bye . . ."

Mr. Machinist lives in Hidden Valley and every Halloween he hides in his bushes, snapping pictures of kids on his property. Last year he caught some boy soaping up his car windows and besides taking his picture, which he sent to the police, he also turned the hose on him. Mr. Machinist has no sense of humor.

After supper I packed a shopping bag with a flashlight, a can of pink Silly String, a roll of toilet paper and my Unicef collection box. In my free hand I carried my flenser sword.

When my parents got home my mother said, "It's freezing out. You can't go like that."

"But if I wear a jacket no one will be able to see my flenser suit."

"Not only do you have to wear a jacket," Mom said, "but it has to be a heavy one . . . zipped up!"

"Oh Mom! You do this to me every Halloween."

"I'm sorry, Jill. It's the weather, not me. Halloween should be in August. Then you wouldn't have to wear anything."

"Ha ha," I said, pulling the pillowcase over my head. I put my flenser hat on top of that.

"Are you sure you can see?" Dad asked me.

"Hold up your fingers and I'll tell you how many," I said.

My father held up two. I said, "Um . . . six . . . right?" Then I laughed. So did Dad.

"Gordon . . . I'm afraid she's going to suffocate in that get-up," my mother said.

"Can you breathe?" Dad asked.

"Yes . . . I can see and I can breathe and Tracy's waiting for me so can I please go now?"

"Have fun," my mother said. "But remember, if you're not home by eight-thirty, I'm sending your father to find you."

"I'll be home . . . I promise." I walked to the

front hall and grabbed my heavy jacket from the closet. Kenny was standing at the door, waiting for Trick-or-Treaters. He never goes out on Halloween night. He says it's because he likes to answer the doorbell, handing out the candy and Unicef money, but I know the truth. Kenny is chicken. He's scared of the dark. He really believes in witches and goblins and monsters. That's why he sleeps with his closet light on every night.

I took three nickels from the bowl on the hall table.

"Hey . . ." Kenny said. "That's Unicef money."

"I know it!" I dropped the nickels into my collection box. "Bye, chicken . . . watch out for the wolf-man . . . he just loves Halloween!" I snorted and jumped away as Kenny tried to slug me.

It was a very dark night. There was no moon and there aren't any street lights in our neighborhood.

"I think we should head straight for Hidden

Valley," Tracy said. "There aren't enough houses to bother with around here."

"Agreed."

We took turns holding the flashlight. Mrs. Wu had made Tracy wear a heavy jacket too. All you could see of her Big Bird suit was a bunch of yellow feathers hanging out. She had her pillowcase over her head, same as me, but she had taped a few feathers to the top, sort of like an Indian headdress.

When we got to Hidden Valley it was easier to see because most families there have lamp posts down by the road. "You brought the eggs, didn't you?" I asked Tracy.

"Yes . . . six of them."

"Do they smell bad?"

"I don't know. When we crack them we'll find out. They should be rotten by now. I've had them in my dresser drawer for a month."

"Good."

There are some things I would never do on Halloween. I would never smash a carved pumpkin. I know how that feels because last year somebody swiped both pumpkins off our front porch and smashed them all over the road. This year me and Kenny got smart. We put our pumpkins in the window, where they'll be safe. Also, I would never mess around with little kids, trying to steal their loot. That's mean.

But nothing is too mean for Mr. Machinist, which is why Tracy and I planned to crack eggs in his mailbox. He deserves it. He won't give to Unicef and if ever there was a person who'd put razor blades in apples it's him.

I'm not allowed to eat much of anything I collect Trick-or-Treating, especially apples. Mrs. Sandmeier makes them all into applesauce. So far she's never found a razor blade but my mother says there are crazy people all over and she isn't taking any chances.

Mr. Machinist's mailbox is next to his driveway, by the side of the street. It says MACHINIST in small stencilled letters.

Tracy took out an egg and handed it to me. "Ready for action?"

I looked around, sure that Mr. Machinist was lurking behind a tree, just waiting to jump out and snap my picture. But I didn't see anything so I said, "I guess so . . ."

Tracy took another egg out of her bag and held it herself. "You go first," she told me.

I put my shopping bag and sword on the ground. Then I opened Mr. Machinist's mailbox. It squeaked.

"Go ahead," Tracy whispered. "Do it."

I expected a flashbulb to pop in my face as I cracked the egg and dumped it inside. The yolk broke and dripped all over. "Now you go," I told Tracy.

Tracy cracked her egg and threw it inside the box too. We looked at each other, then reached for two more eggs and did the same thing again. When we came to the last eggs we didn't bother cracking them first. We just tossed them into the mailbox, shell and all. After that we picked up our things and ran as fast as we could.

When we were far enough away we started to laugh. "We did it!" I said. "We really did it."

"And they were rotten," Tracy said. "Did you get a whiff?"

"Yeah . . . they were just great!"

"Won't he be surprised tomorrow when he reaches in for his mail . . ."

"And comes out with a handful of raw, rotten eggs!"

"Oh Mr. Machinist . . ." Tracy sang, "you deserve it!"

After that we went Trick-or-Treating. We stopped at every house in Hidden Valley. At Wendy's we got two miniature Hershey bars and a handful of Unicef pennies. At Caroline's we each got a quarter for Unicef and a napkin full of chicken corn. At Robby Winters' his mother invited us inside while she wrote a one-dollar check for each of us to give to Unicef.

"I never got a check before," Tracy said, when we were outside again.

"Me neither, but I think it's neat."

"So do I."

When we got to Linda Fischer's house Tracy asked, "Do you want to ring her bell?"

"No . . . let's do her trees instead."

"Good idea," Tracy said.

I whipped out the roll of toilet paper and me

and Tracy wound it all around the Fischers' trees. Then we ran up and down the front walk, squirting pink Silly String on all the bushes. I was having the best time. I wished Halloween came more than once a year. I shook the can and aimed it at the hedge right next to the house. "A person gets what she deserves," I sang. But when I pushed the button nothing came out of the can. "It's empty," I told Tracy.

"So's mine," she said.

We raced down the driveway. Tracy had a piece of blue chalk with her and she snapped it in half and both of us laughed like crazy as we wrote *Blubber lives here* all over the street.

Wendy and Caroline came along then, shining their flashlights in our faces. "Hey," I said, "turn those things off."

"Who are you?" Wendy asked.

"Who do you think? It's me, Jill."

"Prove it," Wendy said.

I took off my hat and pillowcase.

"Oh, it really is you," Wendy said. "Is that Tracy?"

"Naturally."

"We smashed six pumpkins," Caroline said.

"I don't think it's fair to smash pumpkins," I said.

"Fair or not fair, it was great fun," Wendy told me.

"Yeah . . ." Caroline said. "I'll bet you two didn't have such a good time."

"We did too . . . we had a better time," I said.

"Doing what?" Wendy asked.

"Me and Tracy put six eggs in Mr. Machinist's mailbox."

"You did not," Wendy said.

"We did too."

"I don't believe you."

"We can prove it, can't we, Tracy?"

"Yeah . . . we'll show you."

"Wait a second. I've got to get my pillow-case on straight," I said. As I was adjusting it I looked up. And there was Linda, in an upstairs window, watching everything. "Hey . . . there's Blubber!"

"What a chicken," Caroline said, ". . . inside on Halloween night."

"Come on," Tracy said, "let's get out of here."

We raced to Mr. Machinist's house and when we got there I pulled his mailbox open while Tracy lit it with her flashlight.

"Well," I said, "there's the evidence!"

"You really did it." Wendy sounded surprised.

"We told you," I said.

Suddenly a man jumped out from behind a tree. "Hold it right there!" he called.

"Run!" Wendy hollered and she and Caroline took off in one direction while me and Tracy ran in the other.

"Don't look back," Tracy said, breathing hard. "He's got a camera."

"And a hose," I told her, as the water hit me.

When I got home I sneaked in the back door and ran for my bedroom, where I changed into my robe. Then I scooped up the pile of wet clothes from the floor and carried it to the laundry room. I tossed everything into the dryer. Just as I was about to turn it on my mother walked in.

"Oh, hi honey . . . did you have fun?"

"Yes," I said, "lots."

"I didn't know it was raining out."

"It's not."

"Then how come your clothes are in the dryer . . . and your hair's all wet?"

"Oh, that . . ." I said, touching my head.

"Or shouldn't I ask?"

"I really wish you wouldn't," I told Mom.

She smiled and shook her head. Then we went into her bathroom and she dried my hair with her blow-dryer.

6

"The worms crawl in,
the worms crawl out . . ."

On Friday mornings, Miss Rothbelle, the music teacher, comes to our classroom. She is tall and skinny with two circles of rouge on her cheeks, hair that is practically blue and fingernails like Dracula. Next to her Mrs. Minish looks like Miss America.

I don't know if Miss Rothbelle has just one dress or a lot of dresses exactly alike, but she always looks the same. And every time I pass her in the hall, instead of saying hello, Miss Rothbelle blows her pitchpipe at me.

Today she said, "We will continue where we left off . . . with lullabies. Remember, you're going to sing at assembly next week and I want a perfect performance. So listen carefully." She blew into her pitchpipe, then tuned herself up by humming one note until she was satisfied. Her voice is like an opera singer's but it cracks on the high notes.

"Sweet and low . . . sweet and low . . ." Miss Rothbelle sang, walking around the room. When she came to Robby Winters she gave his ear a tug and he sat up straight and tall. Then she tapped Irwin on the head with her ballpoint pen and he put away his comic.

"Low . . . low . . . breathe and blow . . ."

I folded my hands on my desk as Miss Rothbelle came closer to me.

"Sleep my little one . . . sleep my little one . . ."

It's very hard to keep a straight face when Miss Rothbelle is singing, especially when she's singing "Sweet and Low" and comes to the line about "mother's breast." She always trills the *br.*

I held my breath until Miss Rothbelle passed my desk.

When she finished her song she was right

next to Wendy. "Wendy . . . can you tell me what was coming out of my mouth as I sang?"

"Out of your mouth?" Wendy asked.

"That's right," Miss Rothbelle told her.

"Well . . . it was . . . um . . . words?"

"No . . . no . . . no . . ." Miss Rothbelle said.

Wendy was surprised. She can always give teachers the answers they want.

Miss Rothbelle moved on. "Do you know, Caroline?"

"Was it sound?"

"Wrong!" Miss Rothbelle said, turning. "Donna Davidson, can you tell me?"

"It was a song," Donna said.

"Really Donna . . . we all know that!" Miss Rothbelle looked around. "Linda Fischer, do you know what was coming out of my mouth as I sang to the class?"

Linda didn't say anything.

"Well, Linda . . ." Miss Rothbelle said.

"I think it was air," Linda finally told her. "Either that or breath."

Miss Rothbelle walked over to Linda's desk. "That was not the correct answer. Weren't you paying attention?" She pulled a few strands of Linda's hair.

A loud noise came out of Linda then. At first I wasn't sure what it was but then the smell hit me and I knew. I wondered if she'd had sauerkraut for breakfast because that happens to Kenny whenever he eats it.

Miss Rothbelle made a face and stepped away.

I bit my lip to keep from laughing. With Mrs. Minish you can laugh out loud and nothing really bad happens. She threatens to send us to Mr. Nichols' office but she never does. With Miss Rothbelle you don't laugh, no matter what.

She walked up and down the aisles until she stopped at my desk. "You're smiling," she said.

"I am?"

"You are."

"I don't think so, Miss Rothbelle," I said.

"We'll see if you've been paying attention . . . suppose you tell me the answer to my question."

I had no idea what Miss Rothbelle wanted me to say. There was just one thing left that could have been coming out of her mouth as she sang, so I said, "It was spit."

"What?" Miss Rothbelle glared at me.

"I mean, it was saliva," I told her.

Miss Rothbelle banged her fist on my desk. "That was a very rude thing to say. You can sit in the corner for the rest of the period."

I pressed my lips together and felt my face turn hot as I carried my chair to the front of the room. I sat down facing the blackboard. Damn that Blubber! I thought. It's all her fault. She's the one who made me smile with her disgusting smell. Miss Rothbelle never would have called on me if I hadn't been smiling. Blubber's the one who should be sitting in the corner. I'd like to tell that to Miss Rothbelle. I really would. Talk about unfair . . .

At the end of music period Robby Winters called out, "Miss Rothbelle . . . Miss Rothbelle . . ."

"What is it?" she asked.

"You never told us what was coming out of your mouth when you sang."

"That's right," Miss Rothbelle said. "I didn't."

"What was it?" Robby asked.

"It was melody," Miss Rothbelle said. Then she spelled it. "M-e-l-o-d-y. And every one of you should have known." She blew her pitch-pipe at us and walked out of the room.

At eleven Mr. Kubeck, the custodian, delivers our lunch milk. He leaves it outside the class-room door, in the hall. When I see it standing there my stomach growls and I start thinking about my peanut butter sandwich, sitting inside my stuffy old locker, getting soggy. By lunchtime the milk is warm. I think it's sour too. I've told my mother to report that to the Board of Health. We'll be able to buy cold milk next year, when the school gym is converted into a part-time cafeteria. Until then we have to suffer through lunch in our classrooms.

At noon Mrs. Minish leaves the room. She goes out to lunch every day. All the teachers do. It makes me mad to think of them sitting in some nice restaurant eating hamburgers and french fries while I have to sit at my desk drinking sour milk.

As soon as Mrs. Minish is gone we all move our desks around. I push mine next to Wendy's. So does Caroline. Sometimes Donna Davidson joins us and other times she sits across the room with Laurie, which is fine with me. I can't stand hearing her horse stories.

Linda Fischer eats by herself. I watched as she unpacked her lunch and spread it out across her desk. She had a sandwich, a pack of Hostess cupcakes and a big red apple.

"You're going to turn into a real whale if you keep eating like that," Wendy told her.

"Just shut up," Linda said, more to her sandwich than to Wendy.

"Well, listen to that!" I said. "Blubber told Wendy to shut up. Can you imagine!"

"Some people don't know how to talk nice," Caroline said.

"Didn't your mother teach you any manners, Blubber?" Wendy asked.

"I don't think so," I said. "Otherwise Blubber wouldn't chew with her mouth open."

"Oh yes," Wendy said. "I noticed that too. She must want us to see that she has an egg-salad sandwich."

"On whole wheat bread," Caroline added.

"And how lovely it looks all chewed up in her mouth," I said. "I guess that's why she decided to report on the whale. She has a lot in common with them." I was beginning to enjoy myself.

"Blub . . . blub . . . blub . . ." Wendy made this funny noise.

Linda took her cupcakes and stuffed them back into her lunch bag. She stood up and headed for the trash basket but Wendy stopped her before she could throw anything away. "You can't waste those *beautiful* cupcakes, Blubber!"

"I'll take them," Robby Winters called.

Wendy grabbed the bag out of Linda's hand, took out the package of cupcakes and threw it across the room to Robby. He tossed it to Bill, who passed it to Michael. Michael ate one. The other cupcake was squashed by that time but Irwin stuffed it into his mouth anyway.

Linda went back to her desk. Wendy followed her. "Oh look . . . Blubber has a shiny red apple." She held it up for the class to see. Then she put the apple on top of her head and paraded around the room.

Michael stood on his desk and yelled, "I'm William Tell!"

"Who's he?" Laurie asked.

"The guy who shot the apple off his kid's head, dummy." Michael pretended to pull back his bow and aim an arrow at Wendy's head.

"Help . . . oh help!" Wendy cried, racing around the room, holding the apple on her head with one hand.

"Help is on the way," I called, taking off my shoe and throwing it at Michael. It hit him in the leg. He picked it up and ran to the window.

"You wouldn't!" I yelled.

As soon as I said that Michael raised the window and tossed out my shoe. It landed in the bushes.

"You jerk! You absolute idiot!"

"I'll fix him, Jill," Wendy called, firing the apple at Michael. It missed him and crashed against the blackboard. Bruce picked it up, polished it off on his shirt, then took a bite.

Donna pointed at him and chanted, "He ate the poison apple . . . he ate the poison apple . . ."

"Oh . . ." Bruce made this gurgling noise, clutched his stomach and dropped to the floor. He rolled over and played dead while the rest of us circled around him singing, "The worms crawl in, the worms crawl out, they eat your guts, and they spit them out . . ."

"It's *much* too noisy in here!" Mrs. Horvath stood in our doorway with her hands on her hips. She is in charge of us during lunch. She's called a "lunch teacher" but really, she's more like a policewoman, patrolling the halls and sticking her head in and out of classrooms.

We shut up in a hurry and scrambled back to our desks.

"What is that?" she asked, spying the apple on the floor.

Nobody answered.

"To whom does this apple belong?"

We all looked at Linda.

"Well?" Mrs. Horvath said.

"It's mine," Linda told her in a very weak voice.

"Food does not belong on the floor!" Mrs. Horvath shouted.

"I know," Linda said.

"Then why is it there?"

Linda didn't say anything.

"Do you want me to report you to Mr. Nichols?"

"No."

"Then pick up that apple this instant!"

Linda hurried to the front of the room, picked up the apple and dumped it into the trash basket.

"That's better," Mrs. Horvath said. "Now, get into your jackets and go outside."

As long as it isn't raining we go to the playground after lunch. Rainy days are bad because we have to spend all of lunch hour in our classroom and that is just so boring, even though Mrs. Minish unlocks the supply closet and hands out extra vanilla drawing paper.

I prayed that Mrs. Horvath wouldn't notice I was wearing just one shoe and all the way down the hall I walked with my sock foot in front of my shoe foot. Outside, instead of jumping rope, like usual, I hunted in the bushes for my shoe. As soon as Tracy heard what happened she came over to help. When we finally found it, it was time to go back to class.

7

"Doesn't it stick to the roof of your mouth?"

My mother has decided to give up cigarettes. She says if I have enough will power to stop biting my nails then she should have enough to stop smoking. I'm very proud of her. Dad says we've got to encourage Mom, so Kenny gives her all the bubble gum from his baseball cards. Mom can blow the biggest bubbles I've ever seen. She has to keep her mouth busy so she won't crave cigarettes, which is why she's taken up chewing. I know how she feels, only with me, instead of chewing, I wiggle my loose tooth.

On Sunday night, Mom reminded me that I still have nothing to wear to Warren Winkler's bar mitzvah and it's just two weeks away. His father lived next door to my father when they were boys. We don't see the Winklers very often—just once or twice a year—but that is more than enough for me. Warren is such a creep! His mother is always making jokes about how me and Warren will like each other a lot more when we grow up, which proves that Mrs. Winkler doesn't know anything.

"Do I really have to go?" I asked my mother.

"Yes," Mom said, trying to scrape the bubble gum off her chin.

"You need alcohol for that," I told her.

"Oh . . . thanks."

We went into the bathroom and I watched Mom clean off her face. "I think I'll wear a long dress," I said. "Tracy went to a bar mitzvah last year and she wore one. Her mother made it for her . . . it's beautiful . . . maybe she'd lend it to me."

"That's ridiculous," Mom said.

"What is?" I asked. "Wearing a long dress or borrowing Tracy's?"

"Both."

"Then what am I going to wear?"

"I'll look for something this week."

"No ruffles or anything like that."

"Don't worry. I'll get a very simple dress."

"I hope so," I said.

We always get off to a slow start on Monday mornings because Mrs. Minish has to collect our milk money for the week. I've noticed that she isn't so fast when it comes to arithmetic. If she didn't pay so much attention to thinking the problem through, like it says in our book, she could probably do better.

While Mrs. Minish was counting, Robby Winters came over to my desk, holding his hands out like some kind of zombie. He had a pin stuck through the skin of every finger. I used to think it was very brave of him to do that. But when I tried it myself I found out it's easy. It doesn't even hurt. Last time I did it Mrs. Sandmeier caught me and made me soak my fingers in Epsom Salt for two hours.

"Robby, you are gruesome," I told him, as he pushed his pin fingers in my face. As soon as he saw that he couldn't get anywhere with me he went over to Linda Fischer. She screamed.

Mrs. Minish looked up. "What's going on?"

"It's Robby . . ." Linda said. "He's got pins in his fingers."

"Take them out, Robby," Mrs. Minish said. "Right now."

"But they feel nice," Robby told her.

"Take them out!"

"Yes, Mrs. Minish."

When she was finished with the milk money, Mrs. Minish announced that we would have a social studies test on Wednesday, on the explorers. I get them all mixed up. I can never remember which one is de Vaca and which one is de Soto and who discovered what.

At lunchtime, Wendy and Caroline traded sandwiches. Wendy loves salami and Caroline's favorite is tuna. I had my usual, peanut butter.

"Don't you get sick of the same old thing day after day?" Wendy asked.

"Nope."

"Doesn't it stick to the roof of your mouth?" Caroline said.

"If it does I just work it off with my tongue."

"It's good you're so skinny," Caroline told me. "Peanut butter's fattening."

"Jill doesn't have to worry," Wendy said. "Not like some people . . ."

We all looked over at Linda. She had her lunch spread out on her desk—two pieces of celery, one slice of yellow cheese and a package of saltine crackers. "Hey . . ." I said, "Blubber's on a diet!"

"Is that right?" Wendy asked.

"Yes," Linda said. "I'm going to lose ten pounds and then you won't be able to call me that name anymore."

"What name?" Wendy said, and we all giggled.

"You know."

"Say it!"

"No . . . I don't have to."

Wendy got up and went over to Linda's desk. She made a fist at her. "Say it . . ."

"Blubber," Linda said very low.

"Louder."

"Blubber," she said in her regular voice.

Caroline was laughing like a hyena. I've

never heard a hyena laugh, but I just know it would sound like Caroline. I think she's really stupid sometimes.

"Now say, *My name will always be Blubber*," Wendy told Linda.

"No . . . because it won't."

"Say it!" Wendy told her and she didn't look like she was fooling around anymore.

I sat on the edge of my seat, not moving.

"My name will always be Blubber," Linda said. There were tears in her eyes.

"And don't you forget it," Wendy said, "because even if you weigh fifty pounds you'll still be a smelly whale."

That night, after my bath, I went to my parents' room. Mom was stretched out reading a book. I did a flying leap onto her bed and lay down next to her.

"You're sleepy, aren't you?" she asked, playing with my hair.

"A little . . ."

"You should go to bed."

"In a minute."

"Okay."

"Mom . . ."

"Hum?"

"Remember the time that sixth-grader called Tracy a *chink*?"

"I remember," Mom said.

"And how she socked him right in the nose and he never bothered her again . . ."

"Uh huh."

"Well, that's what I'd do if somebody called me a name."

"I wouldn't," Mom said.

"How come?"

"Because it makes more sense to just laugh it off."

"I never thought of that."

"A person who can laugh at herself will be respected," Mom said.

"Always?"

"Usually . . . what makes you ask, anyway?"

"Nothing special . . . just this girl in our class who lets everybody walk all over her . . . she really looks for it."

"You should try putting yourself in her place."

"I could never be in her place!"

"Don't be too sure," Mom said, as she took off her reading glasses and slid them into their case.

"I think I will go to bed now," I said, leaning over for my kiss.

8

"Pass it on . . ."

On Wednesday morning we had our social studies test on the explorers. It was all matching and multiple-choice questions. Mrs. Minish handed back the corrected test papers right after lunch. I got a C. I knew I'd forget which one was de Vaca and which one was de Soto and I did. I also goofed up Cortez and Mexico. But what got me really sore was that Wendy and Caroline both got A's. And I saw Caroline copy all the answers off Wendy. Sometimes I wish Mrs. Minish would wake up.

Miss Rothbelle sent for us at one-fifteen so we'd have time to rehearse before assembly. She made us stand in size place on the stage. I wound up between Rochelle, who is a new girl, and Linda, with Wendy right behind me. All during rehearsal Wendy kept giving me little pokes and pinches, trying to make me laugh. But I kept a straight face the whole time.

We practiced singing each of our lullabies twice. Miss Rothbelle seemed satisfied and went down to talk to Mr. Vandenberg. He always plays the piano for assemblies. I wish he taught music instead of Miss Rothbelle. He has this funny moustache that he's always twirling and he loves to tell jokes.

As soon as Miss Rothbelle was gone Wendy leaned close and whispered, "Nobody sings *breast* but Blubber. Pass it on . . ."

I whispered that to Rochelle and she whispered it to Donna, who was on her other side.

Then Mr. Vandenburg started playing a march and we watched as all the other classes filed into the auditorium. When everyone was settled Miss Rothbelle blew her pitchpipe at us and we hummed the opening note of "Brahms' Lullaby." We sang two more songs before we got to "Sweet and Low." The way Miss Rothbelle conducted us you'd have thought she was leading some famous symphony.

In the second verse of "Sweet and Low," when we came to the line that goes, "Rest . . . rest . . . on mother's breast . . ." all of us mouthed the word "breast" except Linda. She sang it loud and clear with a trill on the *br*, the way Miss Rothbelle does. It was like a one word solo. The rest of us came back in on the next word but by then most of the kids in the audience were laughing so hard no one could hear us sing. Linda turned absolutely purple.

I might have cracked up right on stage except for my loose tooth. Because all of a sudden it wasn't there anymore. It didn't fall out of my mouth but I could feel it rolling around on my tongue. I didn't know what to do. I was afraid if I let it stay in my mouth I would swallow it, so I spit it into my hand and stuck my tongue in the space where my tooth used to be. I tasted blood.

After the assembly Miss Rothbelle made an

announcement to our class. "Everyone except Linda will stay after school tomorrow . . . and if this ever happens again you will all fail music!"

I knew she'd say something like that.

I showed Tracy my tooth on the way home from school. "It's neat," she said. "How much do you think it's worth?"

"I'm not sure," I told her. "Last time I got a quarter."

"If I were you I'd try for more. We haven't got that many baby teeth left."

"I'll try," I said.

I didn't know which to tell my parents first—that I have to stay after school tomorrow or that I lost my tooth. I decided on the tooth. I handed it to my father.

"Very nice," he said, inspecting it. He passed it to Mom.

"Don't forget to put it under your pillow," she said.

"I won't."

Mom handed the tooth back to me. "I went shopping at lunchtime," she said. "I found the bar mitzvah dress. It's in a box on my bed."

"I hope I like it," I said.

"I hope it fits."

The dress turned out to be a short knitted thing, with tiny sleeves, a round neck, and three stripes on the skirt. "It itches," I told my mother after she'd made me try it on.

"It can't," Mom said. "It's acrylic, not wool."

I wiggled around. "It itches all over."

"There's probably a scratchy tag inside. I'll take it out later."

When Mom and Dad came into my room to kiss me goodnight Mom said, "Did you put the tooth under your pillow?"

I patted my pillow and said, "Of course."

"I hope the Tooth Fairy comes," Dad said.

"Me too. Do you think she could leave me a check this time, instead of cash?"

"A check?" Mom asked.

"Yes." I twisted the edge of my blanket. "Made out to the Winthrop Stamp Company for $2.87."

"That's a lot of money for one little tooth," Dad said.

"I know it," I told him. "But I haven't got many baby teeth left and I'm sure the Tooth Fairy will understand if you explain it to her."

Mom and Dad looked at each other. "We'll try to get the message through," Mom said. "Now go to sleep."

The next morning I felt under my pillow. The tooth was gone and in its place was the check I'd asked for. I found Dad in the kitchen, squeezing oranges, and I thanked him.

Then I went looking for Mom. I heard the water running in her bathroom. I figured she was washing up so I tried the door. It was unlocked. "Mom, thanks for the . . ." I stopped right in the middle. Mom wasn't at the sink. She was crouched in the corner of the bathroom, smoking a cigarette! "Mom . . . what are you doing?"

My mother tossed the butt into the toilet. Then she stood up and fanned the air, trying to get rid of the smoke. "I couldn't help it," she said. "I really needed one this morning."

"You promised . . ." I began.

"I promised to try and I *am* trying!"

"But . . ."

My mother held up her hand. "Please get ready for school. I have a very busy day coming up and I don't have the time to drive you if you miss your bus."

"Oh, that reminds me," I said. "I have to stay after school today."

"Well, this is a fine time to tell me," Mom said, as she pulled on her pantyhose.

"I forgot to tell you last night because. I was so busy trying on the dress and thinking about my tooth and all . . ."

"Damn!" Mom said. "I just got a run. Now I'll have to wear pants."

"And anyway, the whole class has to stay after."

"Why?"

"Oh . . . we were fooling around in music."

Mom went to her closet. "Damn again . . . they're at the cleaners."

"I'll get a ride home with one of the mothers, so don't worry."

"You're sure?" Mom asked, looking for

another pair of pantyhose. "Because I could call a taxi."

"Oh no . . . Wendy said either her mother or Caroline's will drop me off."

"Leave a note for Mrs. Sandmeier."

"I will."

On the way to school I told Tracy about my check and that now I have enough to buy a whole bunch of approvals from Winthrop. When Tracy heard that she started wiggling both of her loose teeth.

9

"So who won the game?"

Mrs. Minish told us to hurry and settle down as we walked into our room because she had to collect the money for our class trip. We're going to the Planetarium next month. I've already been there four times.

I knew it would take Mrs. Minish forever to get our trip money straight so I pulled my chair over to Wendy's desk. She and Caroline had a couple of books spread out in front of them to make it look like they were hard at work on some assignment. But really, they were making up a list. They showed it to me.

How to Have Fun With Blubber

1. Hold your nose when Blubber walks by.
2. Trip her.
3. Push her.
4. Shove her.
5. Pinch her.
6. Make her say, <u>I am Blubber, the smelly whale</u> <u>of class 206.</u>

Before I'd had a chance to read the whole thing the office called on the intercom, asking for a messenger from our class and Mrs. Minish looked up and said, "Jill, will you run down to the office please."

Ms. Valdez—that's what the clerk likes to be called—handed me a notice that had to be signed by all the fifth-grade teachers. By the time I got back to our room my class was saying the Pledge of Allegiance. I waited outside the door until they were through. Bruce picked his nose the whole time, which wasn't a very patriotic thing to do.

After that, it was time to line up for gym. I

like Mr. Witneski, our gym teacher. He treats the girls the same as the boys. This time of year we usually play kickball. I have this great daydream where it's the bottom of the last inning and my team has two outs with the bases loaded. We are losing by three runs and I'm up. When the ball comes rolling toward me I kick it so hard and so fast that it goes way into the outfield, over everyone's head. It's a home run and we win the game. My whole team starts yelling and cheering and then they pick me up and carry me around on their shoulders and after that I'm always the first one picked for a team. So far this has never happened but I keep hoping it will.

While we were walking down the hall Caroline whispered, "You missed a good show. When Blubber went up to give Minish her money, Wendy stuck out her foot and tripped her and Blubber fell flat on her face . . . and Minish said, *From now on try to be more careful, Linda*."

"What'd Blubber say to that?"

"Nothing . . . what do you think?"

* * *

I called Tracy as soon as I got home from school.

"What did Miss Rothbelle make you do?" she asked.

"We had to write, *I was very rude yesterday. I will not misbehave in music again.*"

"How many times?"

"One hundred."

"Ugh!"

"You can say that again. Did you hear about gym?"

"No . . . what?"

"Well . . . Michael and Rochelle were captains."

"Yeah . . ."

"And I was on Michael's team and Wendy and Blubber were on Rochelle's. Blubber was the last one picked."

"That figures."

"So . . . on my first time up I kicked a blooper right at Blubber . . . not on purpose or anything . . . it just happened . . . you know?"

"Yeah . . ."

"And probably anyone else would have just

caught it and I'd have been out. But Blubber missed the ball . . ."

"And?"

"Fell over backwards."

Tracy laughed.

"So then Wendy started yelling at Blubber, *You dummy, you idiot, you smelly whale* . . . because Wendy really likes to win."

"I know."

"So then Blubber started bawling, *It's not my fault* and she grabbed her belly and groaned, *She hit me right in the stomach* . . . *ohhhh!*"

"Then what?" Tracy asked.

"So Mr. Witneski dashed out to the field and said, *Are you hurt, Linda?* which made Blubber start crying harder. She sounded like a sick elephant. And the whole time she kept telling Mr. Witneski that I did it on purpose . . . that I aimed right for her . . . as if I could just kick the ball wherever I wanted."

"Fat chance," Tracy said.

"Which is what I told Mr. Witneski."

"Did he believe you?"

"I'm not sure because then he turned to me, of all people, and I was already safe at second base . . . and he said, *Jill, take Linda down to see the nurse, please.*"

"Oh no!"

"Oh yes! But I told him, *Mr. Witneski, I'm on base.*"

"So he didn't make you go?"

"Wrong! He said, *Someone can run for you* and next thing I know Caroline was sent in to take my place. And I was stuck walking the smelly whale to the nurse's office."

"Go on . . . go on . . ."

"Well . . . first thing she says is, *Why do you always pick on me?* So I tell her, *I don't pick on you* and she goes, *You do too. You and all your friends. And I never did anything to you.* So I tell her, *You're full of it* and she goes, *Some day you'll be sorry. I'll get you for this.* So I tell her, *I'm really scared* and she goes, *You should be.* So I say, *Yeah . . . I'm shaking all over* and then she goes, *I hate you!*"

"She really said that?" Tracy asked.

"Yup. So then we get to the nurse's office

and she starts bawling all over again and the nurse asks her where it hurts and Blubber tells her, *In my stomach* and the nurse makes her lie down on the cot and pops the thermometer in her mouth even though I say, *She got hit with a ball. She doesn't have a temperature.* But the nurse doesn't care what I say because she likes to stick thermometers in people's mouths which I happen to know because of that time I sprained my finger and the first thing she did was take my temperature. So while the thermometer is in Blubber's mouth and she can't talk I ask the nurse, *Can I go now?* and she tells me, *Yes, dear . . . and thank you for bringing her.*"

"So who won the game?" Tracy asked.

"Them . . . two to ten."

That night I struggled over my math homework for an hour. I should be great at math since my father is a tax lawyer and my mother works with computers. I don't understand why I have such a hard time with word problems. Dad explained three of them to me but he doesn't set the problems up the way we're supposed to, so even though I got the right answers I knew Mrs. Minish would still mark some of them wrong. But I'd done my best and Mom and Dad always say that's what counts.

The next morning, when Linda got on the bus, she stood next to my seat and said, "You should see my stomach . . . it's all black and blue."

"I'll bet."

"It is. My mother had to take me to the doctor."

"So?"

"He said you knocked the wind out of me."

"I knew I smelled something bad yesterday!" I turned to Tracy and the two of us absolutely cracked up. I guess nobody ever told Linda about laughing it off.

Right after group science Mrs. Minish told the girls to line up alphabetically. "We're going to the nurse's office to get weighed."

Everybody groaned. We get weighed every fall and again every spring. If I had known that today was the day I'd have eaten a huge breakfast and worn my fisherman's sweater. It's the heaviest thing I own.

I was first on line, with Donna Davidson right behind me and Linda behind her. Wendy and Caroline were near the end of the line since their last names start with *R* and *T*.

When we got to the office the nurse said, "Take off your shoes, please." Then she called, "Jill Brenner."

"Right here," I said. I didn't take off my sneakers. I was hoping that the nurse wouldn't notice. Then I'd weigh two pounds more and she wouldn't be able to give me a lecture about being underweight and how I should drink malteds every day.

"Please take off your shoes, Jill."

"I can't."

She gave me a funny look. "Why not?"

"I promised my mother I wouldn't. My feet get cold when I go barefoot."

"It will only be for a minute."

"I'll get sick if I do."

"Jill . . . stop being silly and take off your shoes."

"Oh . . ." I kicked off my sneakers and stepped on the scale.

I hoped it was at least five pounds over-weight.

"Hmmmm . . ." the nurse said, wiggling the marker all around. "Sixty-seven and a half."

I smiled at her to show I was pleased.

She checked the chart. "That's not much of a gain . . . only half a pound since last spring."

"Well," I told her, "I guess I'm just lucky because I'm always eating."

"You should try to build yourself up. I'd like to see you weigh about seventy-two. Why don't you start drinking a malted every day?"

"Okay . . ." I said, stepping off the scale. I have never had a malted in my life but what the nurse doesn't know won't hurt her.

The nurse was pleased with Donna Davidson. She has one of those perfect bodies where everything fits the way it should.

Linda was next. I took a long time getting my shoes back on so I heard everything.

"Are you feeling better, Linda?" the nurse asked.

"Yes."

"Good . . . now, let's see . . . oh my, ninety-one pounds . . . that's too much for your height."

"I have big bones," Linda said.

"Even so, according to my chart you should lose some weight."

"But I'm on a diet."

"Well, that's a step in the right direction. Remember, no sweets."

"I know it."

After lunch we went outside to jump rope and Donna taught everyone this jumping rhyme she used to sing to the fattest counselor at her summer horse camp.

Oh, what a riot
Blubber's on a diet
I wonder what's the matter
I think she's getting fatter
And fatter
And fatter
And fatter
Pop!

Bruce seemed to enjoy jumping to Donna's rhyme best of all. It suits him even more than Linda because he weighs over a hundred pounds and when he jumps his whole body shakes like Jell-O. He's the one who should be on a diet.

Linda didn't wait her turn on line. She ran back inside and didn't come out at all during recess.

10

"Not crazy . . . just different."

"I think you should know that Mr. Machinist is showing everybody in Hidden Valley those pictures he took of you on Halloween night." Wendy told this to me and Tracy on the way home from school. She and Caroline were sitting opposite us on the bus.

Me and Tracy looked at each other. We'd forgotten all about that.

"But don't worry," Wendy said. "He only got the back of you and with the pillowcases over your heads nobody will ever be able to identify you."

"You saw the pictures?" I asked.

"Last night . . . he brought them over himself."

Caroline said, "When he came to my house I told him I didn't know who you were even though Tracy's feathers were hanging out."

"You could see my feathers?" Tracy asked.

"It's all right!" Wendy said, and she gave Caroline a look that made her shut her mouth and turn to the window. "Nobody's going to say anything. Believe me!"

It's important to be Wendy's friend, I thought. I only hope that what she says is true.

When we got off the bus me and Tracy stopped at our mailboxes, the way we do every day. I got a letter from the Superior Stamp Company. Probably the approvals I sent for last month, I thought.

"You don't think Mr. Machinist will find out who we are, do you?" Tracy asked.

"Definitely not," I told her. "You heard Wendy."

"I guess you're right. But from now on every time my doorbell rings I'm going to faint."

"Me too."

"Listen . . . I'll call you later. I've got to go to the dentist this afternoon."

"Maybe he can pull out your loose teeth and then you can ask for a check."

"Maybe."

"Good luck."

"Thanks," Tracy said. "I'll need it."

As soon as I walked into the house Kenny said, "Guess what . . . Mrs. Sandmeier's going to Switzerland on Saturday."

I dropped the mail on the hall table and ran into the kitchen. "It's not true," I said. "You wouldn't leave us."

Mrs. Sandmeier put her arm around me. "Now, now . . . it's only for three weeks."

"Three weeks! We can't live without you for three weeks."

"Of course you can."

"But who'll take care of us?" I asked.

"Oh . . . your mother and father will think of something."

"I don't see why you can't wait until summer . . . when we're away at camp."

"Because my mother's going to be

eighty-five," Mrs. Sandmeier said, "and I want to be there for her birthday."

"Your mother? I never knew you had a mother."

"Everybody has a mother," Kenny said.

I shot him a look. "You know what I mean," I told Mrs. Sandmeier. I never thought of her as somebody's daughter.

"Mama's a wonderful woman. She lives with my sister in Zurich, and I just decided I don't want to miss this birthday."

"I'll bet they get Grandma to come," Kenny said, shoveling in a handful of potato chips.

"Oh no!" I said. "Not Grandma for three weeks!"

"Or they could call the Carol Agency," Kenny told me.

"What's that?"

"It's the biggest baby-sitting organization in the world. It's in Los Angeles. They have eight hundred registered baby-sitters working for them."

"Why would Mom call a California agency when we live in Pennsylvania?"

"I don't know."

"Kenny Brenner . . . your facts are driving me up the wall!" I went to my room. If Grandma comes I'm moving to Tracy's for three weeks. Grandma makes me so nervous I get diarrhea just from being around her. One time, when my mother couldn't find anyone else to watch us, Grandma moved in for a week. And she wouldn't let me or Kenny do any of the things we always do, like ride bicycles or roller skate, because she thought we'd get hurt. Another thing that got me really sore was the way Grandma made me wear a hat and mittens when it was positively roasting out.

I sat down at my desk and opened the letter from the stamp company. It said:

Dear Friend,

What's wrong? We have noticed that your last few purchases from our approvals have averaged less than 35 cents a selection. We certainly do not want to waste your time by submitting

selections of stamps that have such little
interest to you.

So let's hear from you. Tell us what
type of selections would interest you.
Please use the reverse side of this note for
your suggestions.

Sincerely,
The Superior Stamp Co,

I turned the letter over and wrote my reply.

Dear Superior Stamp Company,
   If you got 50 cents allowance a week
you'd have trouble ordering a lot of stamps
too. Besides, you are not the only stamp
company I deal with. You are not even my
favorite. Half the stamps you send don't
go in my Master Global Album. So you are
lucky to get any business from me.

Unsincerely,
Jill Brenner

The second my mother and father got home I asked, "Is Grandma coming when Mrs. Sandmeier goes to Switzerland?"

Mom wriggled out of her coat.

"And how come you didn't tell us Mrs. Sandmeier's taking a vacation?" I followed Mom into her bedroom.

"Because she wanted to tell you herself," my mother said. "Nothing was definite until yesterday. Please, Jill . . . I'd like to take my shower and then we'll talk about it . . . okay?"

I nodded and waited on Mom's bed. When the water stopped running I stood outside the bathroom and asked, "Is Grandma coming . . . yes or no?"

My mother opened the bathroom door. She had a towel wrapped around her middle and was brushing her hair. "No . . . I don't think she's up to spending three weeks with us."

I looked away and smiled. I couldn't help it. "Then who is?" I asked.

"Who is what?"

"Who's going to take care of us?"

"Great Maudie."

"Great Maudie!" I couldn't believe it. Great Maudie is Grandma's sister but they are complete opposites. They haven't talked to each other in ten years, ever since Great Maudie moved in with her friend, Alfred. "She's really coming?"

"Uh huh. I spoke to her this morning."

"Is Alfred coming too?" He is a very good magician. He has this one trick where he cuts a grapefruit open and there's a dollar bill inside it.

"Alfred can't get away from work so Great Maudie will come without him."

"What will Grandma think?"

"Well . . ." Mom said, "I don't see why she has to find out. She's in Pittsburgh and Great Maudie is in New York. Hand me my robe, please . . ."

I went to Mom's closet and pulled down her favorite robe. It's pink and there's a hole in one sleeve. I gave it to her, then went into the living room.

Kenny and my father were playing chess.

"Did you hear who's coming?" I asked. "Great Maudie."

Kenny nodded and moved his bishop.

I stood over my father's chair. "I thought she's supposed to be crazy," I said, while I scratched his back. My father just loves to have his back scratched.

"Not crazy . . ." he said, "just different . . . mmm . . . that feels good."

"Because my nails are growing!" I showed him. "See . . . they're almost past the tips of my fingers."

Tracy called later. "No news is good news," she said. "Mr. Machinist didn't show up."

"And if he hasn't found out who we are by now we're safe," I told her.

"I think you might be right," Tracy said.

And then both of us added, "I hope," at the same time.

11

"I just can't believe my class would do such a thing."

School isn't as boring as it used to be. Wendy and Caroline made copies of their *How to Have Fun With Blubber* list and on Monday morning they passed them out.

We made Linda say, *I am Blubber, the smelly whale of class 206.* We made her say it before she could use the toilet in the Girls' Room, before she could get a drink at the fountain, before she ate her lunch and before she got on the bus to go home. It was easy to get her to do it. I think she would have done anything we said. There are some people who just make you want to see how far you can go.

Two days later she was saying *I am*

Blubber, the smelly whale of class 206 without anyone forcing her to. She said it *before* she got a drink at the fountain, *before* she went to the toilet, *before* she got on and off the bus, and during lunch, she said it *before* she started eating.

"Very good," Wendy told her. "For that you get a reward. You get to kiss Bruce Bonaventura."

Bruce wasn't all that willing to get kissed, which is why Robby and Irwin had to chase him around the room and then hold him down while Wendy and Caroline dragged Linda over to him.

Bruce said, "If she touches my lips I'll spit at her . . . so help me, I will!"

So we had to settle for Linda kissing Bruce on the cheek. If you ask me she enjoyed it.

On Thursday we made Linda show the boys her underpants. She wasn't anxious to do that so Caroline had to hold her hands behind her back while Wendy lifted her skirt.

Irwin found some names for Linda in the Random House Dictionary, which Mrs. Minish keeps in the corner on its own table. He's really good at looking things up. He can tell you exactly on what page certain words are found. We called Linda "flubsy," "carnivore" and "bestial." I didn't recognize any of them, but they all sounded good.

On Friday, Wendy brought a small piece of chocolate to school, wrapped in gold foil. It came from a box of Barricini's somebody had brought her mother. Wendy showed it to Linda after lunch. "My father had to go all the way to New York for this chocolate-covered ant."

All of us gathered around Linda's desk. Wendy unwrapped the chocolate. She held it close to Linda's face. "You're going to eat this ant, Blubber."

"No I'm not . . . and you can't make me," Linda said.

"Want to bet?" Wendy asked.

"I could get sick and die and then you'd be in big trouble."

"I'm willing to take that chance," Wendy told her.

Linda mashed her lips together and moved

her head from side to side, all the time making noises that sounded like she was smothering to death.

Wendy handed me the candy. Then she said, "Grab her hands, Caroline."

It's good that Caroline's so strong because Linda was really wiggling around. Once Caroline had Linda's hands behind her back Wendy pinched Linda's nose which made her open her mouth. As soon as she did I shoved in the chocolate.

"Now chew and swallow!" Wendy told her, putting one hand over Linda's mouth so she couldn't spit anything out.

Linda kept her eyes shut and we could see her chewing, then swallowing the candy. Wendy let go of her then and sang, "Blubber ate an ant . . . Blubber ate an ant . . ."

We all joined in, making a circle around Linda. Even Rochelle, who usually doesn't pay any attention to the rest of us, was enjoying the show.

But after a minute Linda turned this awful greenish color, gave a big burp, then puked all over her desk and the floor. Wendy ran down the hall for Mrs. Horvath.

When Mrs. Horvath saw the mess she told the boys to get the custodian.

By then Linda was crying. "They made me eat an ant."

"Try to stay calm," Mrs. Horvath told her. "I'll take you down to the nurse's office."

If you throw up in school you automatically get sent home for the rest of the day. So Linda didn't come back to class that afternoon. Instead, Mr. Nichols came to see us.

"We seem to have a little problem, Mrs. Minish," he said, pretending he was talking just to her but looking at all of us. "Linda Fischer said your class made her eat a chocolate-covered ant. In fact she claims they forced it down her throat, causing her to vomit."

"Well . . . this comes as a surprise to me, Mr. Nichols," Mrs. Minish said. "I just can't believe my class would do such a thing."

"Neither can I," Mr. Nichols said. "Nevertheless . . ."

I wondered if something like this could go down on your permanent record card and keep you out of college.

"I'm sure there's a reasonable explanation, Mr. Nichols," Mrs. Minish said. "Can anyone tell us what happened?"

Wendy raised her hand.

"Yes, Wendy?"

"I think I can explain," Wendy said. "You see, Linda's been on this diet and all she eats is cheese and celery . . . so naturally I knew better than to offer her a piece of my candy." Wendy looked at Mrs. Minish.

"Go on," Mrs. Minish said.

"Well . . . Linda just went crazy. I mean, she wanted my candy in the worst way . . . so I told her it was a chocolate-covered ant . . . I thought she wouldn't want to eat it when she heard that." Wendy paused and looked around.

"Yes . . ." Mr. Nichols said.

"But Linda didn't believe me . . . so I told her how my father goes all the way to New York to get these special chocolate-covered

110

ants that my family loves and that they're very fattening. But she still didn't believe me so finally I gave her a piece of my candy and after she ate it I asked her how the ant tasted and that's when she got sick all over the place."

"So it wasn't an ant?" Mr. Nichols asked.

"No, it was regular chocolate candy from Barricini's."

"I see."

"Linda has a lot of imagination," Wendy said.

Only Wendy could sit there telling lies to Mr. Nichols as if he were a regular person instead of the principal of our school.

"I knew there had to be an explanation," Mrs. Minish said.

"Yes . . . well . . ." Mr. Nichols began. "Thank you for your cooperation in this matter."

"Anytime," Mrs. Minish told him, as he walked out of the room.

It was drizzling when me and Tracy stopped for our mail that afternoon. There was nothing for either one of us so we ran home.

"We've got to take the dogs to the vet

today," Tracy said. "I'll see you tomorrow."

"Not tomorrow," I told her. "We're going to a bar mitzvah."

"Oh . . . I forgot about that."

"See you Sunday."

"Right."

When my parents got home my father said he'd had a really rough day and would I mind scratching his back for a little while. I told him I'd love to and that my nails would soon be long enough to file. When Mom had finished showering she came into the living room carrying two Bloody Mary's. She handed one to my father, then flopped onto the sofa. "Jill, would you bring me the mail?"

"Sure." I went to the hall table and got it.

Mom sifted through all the letters and sighed. "Bills and more bills." Then she picked up a yellow envelope. "I wonder what this is," she asked, ripping off the tape. When she saw what was inside she said, "Oh God . . ." Then she cursed a couple of times. My mother's not shy about cursing. She doesn't even care if me and Kenny use those words around the house as long as we understand there are some people who don't approve of them. I think that's the reason most of the kids I know love to curse. It's because their parents make a big deal out of those words. With me it's different. I don't have to yell and scream them on the school bus every day since I can say them any old time I feel like it.

"Gordon . . . look at this . . ." Mom passed him a letter. I read it over Dad's shoulder, while I was scratching. It said:

On Halloween night two youngsters put raw, rotten eggs in my mailbox. Interfering with mail and its delivery is a federal offense. One of these youngsters has been identified as your child. I suggest that you contact me immediately.

William F. Machinist

I stopped scratching my father. Mom held up a picture. It showed two kids from the back. They were running. One of them had feathers hanging out of her jacket. The other one had a hand on her head to keep her hat from flying off. It was definitely me and Tracy.

12

"You really got yourself in big trouble."

"We only did it because he's so mean . . . he hates kids . . . he won't even give to Unicef . . ." I told everyone. It was after dinner and Tracy, her mother and father were sitting with me, Mom and Dad in our living room. Mr. Machinist also sent the picture and note to their house.

Tracy was crying.

"You know you did wrong, don't you, girls?" my father asked.

Tracy nodded.

I said, "In one way I know we did wrong, but in another way, he really deserved it."

"We've always tried to teach Tracy right

from wrong," Mrs. Wu said. "We've always trusted her."

That made Tracy cry even harder. "I don't want to go to jail."

I brought her a box of tissues. "You won't let us go to jail, will you, Dad?" I asked.

"Nobody's going to jail," he said. "But you will have to face the consequences."

Mom and Dr. and Mrs. Wu nodded in agreement.

"We'd better call Mr. Machinist," Dr. Wu said, "and see what he has in mind."

My father went to the phone. I couldn't figure out anything from his end of the conversation. Mr. Machinist must have been doing most of the talking.

"What did he say?" my mother asked when Dad hung up.

"He said he'll talk to the police unless the girls admit what they did and show him that they're sorry."

"Show him that we're sorry . . . how?" I asked.

"He's already cleaned out his mailbox," my

father said, ". . . it's too late for that. But he's got a yard full of leaves that have to be raked up and bagged."

With all the trees in Hidden Valley Mr. Machinist must have millions of leaves, I thought—maybe even billions.

"When?" my mother asked.

"He wanted them to come tomorrow but I explained that we're busy so we settled on Sunday," Dad said.

"Sunday!" I shouted. "That's my only free day this week. Do you think that's fair?"

"I think so," Mom said. "After all, he could have called the police first."

"I think it's fair too," Mrs. Wu said.

"And . . ." my father added, "maybe this way you'll both learn that it's not up to you to decide who deserves what in this world."

After Tracy and her parents were gone, I went upstairs to get ready for bed. Kenny was in the bathroom, brushing his teeth. When he finished spitting he said, "I heard the whole thing. You really got yourself in big trouble."

"Mind your own business," I told him. "And

wipe that blob of toothpaste off the counter."

Kenny ran his towel along the countertop. "I hope you like raking up leaves. If you'd stayed home like me you wouldn't be in this mess."

"Oh . . . shut up, you dumb ass, before I bash your face in!"

I heard him laughing all the way to his room.

When I got into bed I thought about who had identified us. It must have been Blubber! She threatened to get me and she did.

13

"You can't go around scratching all day."

We were late starting out for the bar mitzvah because of Kenny. He didn't want to wear a tie and jacket. "If I can't go in play clothes then I'll just stay home!" he said.

My father doesn't yell often, but when he does you can hear him as far as Tracy's house, maybe even farther. Afterwards he is hoarse for days and has to drink tea with honey. Kenny got the message and put on his new tie and jacket, complaining the whole time that he couldn't swallow and might even choke to death.

I was ready long before anyone else and while they were rushing around I was in the

kitchen, making myself a peanut butter sandwich, just in case I didn't like the bar mitzvah
lunch. I wrapped it in silver foil and put it in
my shoulder bag.

By the time we got to the temple in New
Jersey it was after eleven. There was no place
to park so Dad dropped us off in front while he
drove around the block.

The temple sat on top of a hill and as we
climbed the steps leading to it Mom said,
"Listen, Jill . . . you can't go around scratching
all day. It doesn't look nice."

"I can't help it," I said. "You're the one who
picked out this itchy dress."

"It's too late to do anything about that now.
Try and keep your mind on something else."

"I'll try," I said, but as soon as Mom looked
away I gave myself a quick scratch.

"We just climbed up thirty-seven steps,"
Kenny announced, when we reached the top.

Only Kenny would think of counting!

"Whew . . ." Mom said. "No wonder I'm
winded." She pushed the door open and we
walked inside.

I looked all around. "Wow . . . this is some big place."

"It certainly is," Mom said. "It's enormous."

"Yeah . . . but it's not the biggest synagogue in the world," Kenny told us. "The biggest synagogue in the world is in New York. It's on Fifth Avenue and it's called Temple Emanu-El. It holds six thousand people."

"Tell the little computer to keep his facts to himself today . . . please, Mom."

"Kenny's facts are very interesting," Mom said.

"Yeah . . ."

"Not to me," I told him.

"Stop arguing . . . we've got to find the sanctuary," Mom said. "We're late enough now."

We walked all around before we came to a man standing in a doorway. He had rosy cheeks and a flower in his buttonhole. He smiled at Mom and handed her a prayerbook. Then he put his finger to his lips as if me and Kenny didn't know enough to be quiet. We followed Mom into the sanctuary.

Warren was on the stage. He looked as

creepy as ever, except for his hair. That looked worse. Usually it hangs into his eyes but today it was parted and looked like it had been sprayed.

As soon as he noticed us tiptoeing into the sanctuary he stopped reciting, right in the middle of a prayer. Everyone turned around to see who Warren was watching. My mother tried to smile but as she took a seat in the last row she dropped her pocketbook. It has a chain handle so when it hit the floor it made a clinking noise. Mom bent down and picked it up. She had this funny look on her face. I recognized it right away. It meant *I don't think I can live through this without a cigarette.* I'm very good at knowing what my mother is thinking.

Warren went back to his prayer but he must have lost his place because he stumbled along until the Rabbi pointed and said a few words. I was really surprised that Warren could read Hebrew at all. The last time he was over I showed him my book, *Poems for the John* and he had trouble with every word over two syllables, and that was in English!

When my father walked into the sanctuary a few minutes later, Warren stopped again. This time when everyone turned around there was a lot of whispering. Dad sat down next to me and I could tell he was embarrassed because the back of his neck turned red. That's when Kenny started to sneeze. He never sneezes once like a normal person—it's always twenty or thirty times in a row.

I knew that I shouldn't laugh. I also knew that if I looked at Kenny I would. So I stared straight ahead, right at the back of some girl's head. It reminded me of Linda Fischer's. It was the same potato shape and the hair was the same too—reddish-brown and curled up at the edges.

At least that gave me something to think about so I didn't have to listen to Warren's stupid speech which was something about being grateful to everyone he knew.

After the service we went to a party at Mr. Winkler's country club. As soon as we walked into the lobby this woman asked us our names.

"Brenner," Dad told her.

"Oh yes," she said, fishing some little white cards out of a pile. She handed them to my father. He passed one to me and one to Kenny.

"What's this?" Kenny asked.

"It tells you what table to sit at for lunch," Mom said.

"You mean me and Kenny can't sit with you?" I asked.

"We're at Table Nineteen," Dad told me.

"I'm at Table One," Kenny said.

I looked at my card. "I'm at Table One, too."

"All the young people are probably sitting together," Mom said.

"But I'd rather sit with you," I said. "Suppose I don't like what they have to eat?"

"Just say *no, thank you*," Dad told me. "Nobody's going to force you to eat anything."

"You should have brought your peanut butter!" Kenny laughed. "Then you wouldn't have to worry."

"Shut up, you little brat!"

"It won't hurt you to try something new," my father said.

"Look, Jill . . ." Mom told me, "you don't have to eat a thing. If you're hungry, that's your problem. Now, I'm going to the Ladies' Room . . . do you want to come?"

"All right." I didn't want to stand around talking about food anymore. I was glad I'd brought a secret sandwich with me.

On the way to the Ladies' Room we passed a big room filled with round tables. In the center of each one was a bunch of blue and white flowers.

"Look at that!" I said. "Blue daisies . . . I didn't know there was such a thing."

"They're dyed," Mom said.

"They are?"

"To match the tablecloths."

"This is some party," I said. "I'll bet Warren will get a ton of presents."

"I suppose so . . ."

"Hundreds, I'll bet."

"Probably."

"He's lucky. I wish I could get bar mitzvahed."

"That doesn't necessarily mean big parties and lots of presents, Jill."

"It doesn't?"

"No . . . it's the ceremony that counts, the tradition of reading from the Torah."

"Oh."

We went into the Ladies' Room and took booths next to each other. I watched my mother's feet. It looked like she was dancing.

When we came out there was a woman standing in front of the mirror, putting on lipstick. And next to her was the girl with the potato-shaped head. Only this time I didn't see *just* the back of her head—I saw her whole face in the mirror, including her gray tooth, which is why I suddenly sucked in my breath.

"What's the matter?" Mom asked.

I shook my head a little and whispered, "Nothing." I should have known there couldn't be two heads exactly alike. I should have known it was Blubber.

"I have to fix my hair," Mom said. She stood next to the other woman, who must have been Mrs. Fischer.

Linda turned around and faced me then. We stared at each other. I could tell that she was just as surprised to see me as I was to see her. Neither one of us spoke.

Mrs. Fischer finished with her lips and started in on her eyes. Mom isn't fussy about anything but her hair. She held a pocket mirror up so she could see the back of it. When she was satisfied she put her comb away and took out a little jar of lip gloss. She rubbed some into her lips. It made them shine. Then she turned to Mrs. Fischer and said, "You look so familiar . . . have we met?"

I wanted to grab my mother's hand and pull her out of the Ladies' Room before it was too late. Of all people, why did she have to start up with Mrs. Fischer?

"I was just thinking the same thing," Mrs. Fischer said.

"Where are you from?" Mom asked.

"We live outside of Philadelphia."

"So do we!" Mom said. "In Radnor."

"Well . . . that's how we must know each other. I live there too . . . in Hidden Valley."

"This is a coincidence!" Mom said. "We live right near there . . . off Crestview Drive."

"Isn't this something?" Mrs. Fischer said, "to meet here . . . of all places."

"Are you related to the Winklers?" Mom asked Mrs. Fischer.

"No, Peg was my college roommate."

"And my husband grew up with Harold."

"This is just so funny!"

I didn't think it was funny at all.

"I'm Ann Brenner," Mom said, offering her hand to Mrs. Fischer. "And this is my daughter, Jill."

Mrs. Fischer shook Mom's hand and smiled at me. Any second now they're going to introduce me to Blubber, I thought.

"I'm Janice Fischer and this is my daughter, Linda."

Here it comes!

"You two must know each other," Mom said.

"We do," I mumbled.

"Oh . . . are you the Jill Brenner in Linda's class?" Mrs. Fischer asked.

That did it! "Yes," I said, "but . . ."

"Mom!" Linda tugged at her mother's arm. "Come on . . ."

When they were gone my mother asked, "What was that all about?"

And I told her, "We're not exactly friends."

14

"I'd rather be a skeleton than a whale."

We wound up at Table One, sitting next to each other, of course, and right across the table from Kenny. Everyone else sitting there looked about thirteen. They were all friends of Warren's. None of them spoke to us.

I told Linda, "Just because I'm sitting next to you doesn't mean anything is different. I know what you did." I wanted to let her know I'd figured out she was the one who told Mr. Machinist on me and Tracy. "And just wait till Wendy finds out!"

"Finds out what?"

"You know."

"No, I don't!"

"You're not even a good liar!" I told her.

"Neither are you."

"I'm not lying!"

"Well, neither am I."

The waitress served our first course then. It was chunks of fruit in a pineapple boat. It looked pretty but I don't eat stuff like pineapple in public because the threads get caught in my teeth and make me very uncomfortable. It's the same with celery. I did find two pieces of melon though, before I passed the rest to Kenny.

Next came the soup, which would have been all right except for the vegetables. I don't like vegetables. When Mrs. Sandmeier makes us soup she strains mine so I won't know what I'm eating. Kenny finished my soup too.

While we were waiting for our main course Kenny asked Linda if she believes in ESP. She told him, "Yes . . . and reincarnation too."

"So do I," Kenny said.

Then they had this long conversation about what they were in their other lives and I muttered, *A smelly whale* and Linda said, "If you call me that today I'll tell on you. I really will."

I felt like asking her if Mr. Machinist found out about me and Tracy by ESP or did she meet him face to face and identify us that way?

But Kenny was reciting one of his dumb jokes and right in the middle Linda laughed! I couldn't believe it. I didn't know she knew how.

Our main course was rare roast beef, a tomato stuffed with green peas and funny potatoes in some kind of milky sauce. I hate tomatoes, peas make me choke, and I can't even look at meat with blood dripping out of it. Potatoes in sauce are out of the question. I thought about my peanut butter sandwich and how I might be able to eat it without anyone noticing.

"Don't you eat anything?" Linda asked, after a while.

"Yeah . . ." Kenny told her. "She eats peanut butter."

"Butt out!" I said.

"No wonder you look like a skeleton," Linda said.

"I wouldn't talk if I were you . . . I'd rather be a skeleton than a whale."

"Not me," Kenny said. "Whales are loveable animals . . . skeletons are just dead, bony things."

"Who asked you!"

"You want to share her dinner?" Kenny said to Linda, like I wasn't even there. That fink!

"No, thank you," Linda said. "I've got enough."

"Just a minute," I said. "Who told you I was giving you my dinner?"

"Well, it's just sitting there getting cold," Linda said.

"Yeah, Jill . . ." Kenny told me. "Pass your plate."

"You shouldn't waste good food," Linda said. "Don't you know there are people starving to death in this world?"

"But you're not one of them and neither is my pig of a brother!"

They looked at each other, then at me. "Oh, here . . ." I said, shoving my plate at Kenny.

"What do I care if you wind up with a belly ache." I stood up and went to the Ladies' Room. I was the only one in there besides the attendant. I locked myself into a booth, sat down on the toilet, unwrapped my peanut butter sandwich, and ate it. It made me very thirsty but there was no way I could ask for a cold glass of milk.

Just as I got back to my seat at the table, Kenny yelled, "Hey Warren . . . this is a great party."

One of Warren's friends looked over at Kenny and said, "You're right, kid . . . I'll bet it's the biggest and best party you've ever been to . . . right?"

"Well," Kenny said, "it's big, but it's not the biggest party there ever was."

"I say it is!"

"You're wrong . . . I know all about the biggest party," Kenny said.

Everyone stopped talking and looked over at Kenny.

"Yeah?" Warren's friend said.

"Yeah," Kenny told him.

"I suppose it was at your house." Everybody laughed when Warren's friend said that.

"No," Kenny told them. "It was given by Mr. and Mrs. Bradley Martin of Troy, New York, at the Waldorf Astoria Hotel in New York City."

"And I suppose you were there . . . right?"

"Hardly," Kenny said. "It was in 1897."

Now everybody laughed at Warren's friend.

After all the tables had been cleared the lights dimmed and two men rolled in the biggest birthday cake I'd ever seen. It was shaped like a book. The icing was blue and white. I hoped the inside was chocolate.

"Wow," Kenny said, "that looks delicious."

"Mmmm . . ." Linda licked her lips.

"What about your diet?" I asked. "No sweets . . . remember?"

"My mother said I should eat everything today. It's a special occasion."

"I'll bet that's why your front tooth is gray and rotten," I said, ". . . because you eat too much junk."

"That is not why!"

"Then why is it?"

"Because I ran into a tree and hurt it . . . it's dead."

"The tree?"

"No, my tooth!"

I started to laugh. "Whoever heard of a dead tooth?"

"I did," Kenny said. "But don't worry," he told Linda, "you might grow a whole other set of teeth when you get old. Some people really do."

"They do?" Linda asked.

"Yeah . . . and did you know some babies are born with teeth?"

"They are?" Linda said.

"Kenny!" I gave him a warning look.

He ignored me. "For instance, Louis XIV of France was born with two teeth."

"Nobody's interested, Kenny!" I said.

"I am," Linda told us.

Kenny didn't have time to say anything else because one of the men who had rolled in the cake started blowing into a microphone. I thought maybe he was getting ready to sing "The Star Spangled Banner," like at a ball game, and I wondered if I should stand up. But he didn't sing anything, not even "Happy Birthday." What he did was call up lots of people to light candles on Warren's cake. First Warren's mother and father, then his grandparents, then his aunts and uncles and cousins. The other man had a camera and every time someone lit a candle he snapped a picture.

Then the man with the microphone looked in my direction and said, "Representing the friendship of two old family friends, the Brenners and the Fischers . . . two young ladies will light the thirteenth candle on Warren's cake . . . Jill and Linda."

Both of us were surprised and for a second we didn't move. Finally I pushed my chair back and stood up. Linda followed me. When the man with the microphone held out a lighted candle I took it.

Just as I was about to light the candle on Warren's cake the photographer called, "Hold it . . . let the other girl put her hand on the candle too."

The candle really wasn't big enough for both of us to hold but Linda wrapped her hand around it anyway, forcing my fingers closer to the flame. I was sure I'd wind up getting burned.

"Ready . . ." the photographer called, "now smile . . ."

The flashbulb popped and I couldn't see anything but yellow spots. I let go of the candle to rub my eyes and when I did, Linda lit the one on the cake by herself.

On the way home Kenny announced, "I think Linda Fischer's great. She's been reincarnated six times."

Just to change the subject I told my mother, "I've got a rash all over my behind from this dumb, itchy dress!"

15

"Nobody else had a reason to get us."

"Guess who I saw at Warren Winkler's bar mitzvah?" I asked Tracy the next morning, on our way to Mr. Machinist's house.

"Who?"

"Blubber!"

"No kidding."

"And I had to sit next to her all through lunch."

"Lucky you."

"I'm sure she's the one who told on us, even though she denied it."

"You asked her?"

"Not exactly, but I hinted."

"I don't know," Tracy said. "Plenty of kids in

Hidden Valley could have recognized me by my costume."

"But nobody else had a reason to get us," I said.

"Yeah . . . but if it was Blubber how come she didn't tell on Wendy and Caroline too?"

"They weren't in the picture."

"You could be right," Tracy said.

When we got to Mr. Machinist's house he was outside, waiting for us. We'd rehearsed exactly what we would say to him. Tracy whispered, "One . . . two . . . three . . ." and then we both said, "It was wrong of us to put eggs in your mailbox . . . we're sorry we did it."

"You'd better be," Mr. Machinist said. He wasn't nearly as old as I'd expected. I wondered if he was married or if he lived in that big house all by himself? He showed us the rakes and the bags and then pointed to all the leaves before he went into his house. As if we couldn't find them ourselves.

When he was gone Tracy said, "I think he wears a wig."

"How can you tell?"

"Nobody has hair that thick . . . besides, he didn't have it on straight."

"Wouldn't you love to pull it off?"

"Yes . . . but I'm not going to."

"Me neither."

"He has funny eyes, too."

"I didn't notice."

"Well, I did. They turn down at the corners and they're mean. You can tell a lot about people by staring into their eyes."

By noon we'd been working for three hours and we weren't even halfway through. My mother drove by with lunch for us.

"How are things going?" she asked.

"We'll never finish!" I told her.

"Just do the best you can," she said. "But don't fool around and waste time."

Right after Mom left we decided we had to go to the bathroom. And the more we thought about it the worse we had to go.

"We can ring the bell and ask Mr. Machinist," I said. "He'll have to let us use his bathroom."

"Never," Tracy said. "I'd sooner die than ask

him. I'm going right here." She pointed to the ground.

"Oh, Tracy . . . you can't!"

"Want to bet?" Tracy unbuckled her jeans and started pulling them down.

"Tracy . . . somebody might see."

"How?"

I looked around. Tracy was right. It's very woodsy in Mr. Machinist's side yard. She crouched down next to a big tree. "Ah . . . that feels good," she said.

By that time I had to go so bad I was crossing my legs and shifting my weight from one foot to the other. So I undid my jeans too. I crouched like Tracy and watered a tree. "Oh, Mr. Machinist . . ." I sang softly. "This time you're really getting what you deserve!"

At three o'clock Mrs. Wu drove by with some juice and cookies. I showed her my blisters, one on each finger of my right hand, except for my pinky. Mrs. Wu took the First Aid kit from her glove compartment and rubbed some ointment on my blisters. She gave me enough Band Aids to cover them.

"Your father's coming to pick you up at five," she told me.

"Suppose we're not done by then?" Tracy asked.

"Just do the best you can," Mrs. Wu said. "Nine to five is a long enough working day. Mr. Machinist will have to be satisfied."

We still had two small piles of leaves left when my father pulled up at five. My fingers were killing me and Tracy said she was ready to collapse.

Dad looked around. He said, "You've done a good job, girls. I didn't think you'd get so much done." He walked toward the house and me and Tracy followed. We sat on the front step while my father rang Mr. Machinist's bell.

When the door opened Dad said, "I'm Gordon Brenner and I'm taking the girls home now. They've put in a long hard day and I think you'll agree that they've done a fine job."

"Did they finish?" Mr. Machinist asked.

"Just about."

"Did they learn their lesson?"

Dad looked at me and Tracy.

We nodded.

"I'm sure they have," my father told Mr. Machinist.

"Good . . . that's two more little brats I don't have to worry about . . .

"They are not brats," my father said.

"They are to me." Mr. Machinist slammed his door right in my father's face.

"Damn it," Dad muttered. "He really is a—"

"I told you, didn't I? I told you he deserved to get eggs in his mailbox."

"Hmph . . ." was all my father answered.

When I got home I took a long, hot bath. I ached all over. I was too tired to eat any supper. I wanted to go straight to sleep. But then the phone rang. It was Great Maudie, calling from the station. I'd forgotten she was coming. While Mom drove down to pick her up I got comfortable on the sofa, with the pillow and blanket from my bed.

Great Maudie moved in with one small suitcase and one big carton. When Kenny saw the carton he poked me and grinned. We both thought it was filled with presents for us. So of course we were surprised to find out it was full of food. There were bunches and bunches of carrots—not the kind Mom gets at the supermarket in plastic bags, but the kind that grow in the ground with green tops on them. There was also a whole mess of other vegetable stuff and boxes and jars of funny looking grains.

"Since when are you on a health food kick, Maudie?" Dad asked.

"Six months," Great Maudie said, "and I've never felt better!"

I yawned. Great Maudie sat down beside me. "What you need is vitamins, organically grown food, and plenty of exercise."

"I'm not sick," I said, ". . . just tired."

"Jill's had a hard day," Mom explained.

"Foo . . ." Great Maudie said. "At her age there's no such thing."

Later we found out Great Maudie takes twenty-seven vitamin pills a day.

"Are *you* sick?" I asked. "Is that why you swallow all those vitamins?"

"Just the opposite," Great Maudie said. "They keep me very healthy."

"You should give some to Grandma," Kenny said. "She's always got something wrong with her."

"Her troubles are up here." Great Maudie tapped her head with one finger.

Me and Kenny started laughing because that's what Grandma says about Great Maudie—that she's got something loose in her head.

By the time I went to sleep I decided it would be fun having Great Maudie visit. She laughs a lot. She has a very nice laugh, big and deep.

On Monday morning I changed my mind about her. She had cleaned out our pantry before I woke up. She threw away my Frosted Flakes, Alpha-Bits and Captain Crunch. She made us eat wheat germ mush instead. If this continues, I thought, I might starve to death in three weeks.

16

"If we're going to do this, we're going to do it right."

"Mr. Machinist found out about us," I told Wendy on the bus. She didn't look surprised. "And me and Tracy spent all day yesterday raking his leaves to make up for what we did." I held out my hand and showed her the Band Aids covering my blisters.

"I didn't think she'd do it," Wendy said. "I didn't think she'd have the guts."

"Who?" Caroline asked. "Do what?"

"Who do you think?" Wendy said.

"Blubber?"

"Naturally."

"She told?"

"She'd tell on her own mother," Wendy said.

"Yeah . . ." Caroline agreed. "She probably would."

"We'll get her for this," Wendy told me. "We'll really get her this time."

"I don't want to be in on it," Tracy said. "I promised my parents I'd stay out of trouble from now on."

"Who said anything about trouble?" Wendy asked. "It's just that we can't let her get away with it."

"Count me out," Tracy said. "You can't prove she's the one who told on us."

"Of course she is," Wendy said. "Who else would do it?"

Tracy looked at Wendy and Caroline. Then she shrugged and turned away.

"How dare you accuse us!" Wendy said.

"She's not accusing you . . . are you, Tracy?" I asked.

"I'm not saying anything." Tracy looked out the window.

"If only we could be sure," I tried to explain to Wendy. "I wish we could, but there's no way . . ."

"I don't like what I hear, Jill," Wendy said. "Do you like what you hear, Caroline?"

"Not if you don't," Caroline told Wendy.

"I know," I said after a minute. "I know how we can find out the truth once and for all. We'll have a trial! Just like in real life. With a judge and a jury and everything." I glanced at Wendy to see what she thought of my idea. Personally, I thought it was great.

Wendy smiled. "I'll be the judge," she said. "I'm a very fair person."

I was really glad to hear that Wendy liked my idea.

"Can I be on the jury?" Caroline asked Wendy, as if she was in charge of the whole thing.

"Naturally," Wendy said. "You're my best friend, aren't you."

By the time our bus pulled into the driveway Wendy wasn't mad anymore and everything was settled. She would be the judge, I would be the lawyer and Caroline, Donna, Irwin, Robby and Michael would be on the jury.

"What do you think?" I asked Tracy, as we filed off the bus.

"I think you're scared of Wendy," Tracy answered.

Wendy planned everything. All we had to do was wait for the right moment. The only problem was, Linda didn't come to school that day. And she wasn't on the bus Tuesday or Wednesday morning either.

"She's scared," Wendy said. "She knows we're going to get her and she's scared to come to school."

"The smelly whale's a chicken," Caroline said.

"We've always known that," Wendy told her.

Just as Mrs. Minish was about to take the attendance on Wednesday, Linda came running into the classroom. Wendy flashed me a sign.

"My mother's car wouldn't start," Linda told Mrs. Minish.

"Did you miss the school bus?"

"No . . . my mother's going to drive me to school from now on," Linda said, "and home too."

She really is scared, I thought. She really did tell on us.

At ten o'clock it started to rain. At eleven, when Mr. Kubeck delivered our milk, it was pouring. By noon the playground and field were practically flooded. I knew we wouldn't be able to go outside even if it stopped raining, which it didn't.

As soon as Mrs. Minish left the room for lunch period Wendy passed the word around that we'd have the trial today. We waited until Mrs. Horvath checked our room. "Keep it quiet," she told us. "No talking above a whisper."

"Yes, Mrs. Horvath," Wendy said.

Robby got up and looked out into the hall. He gave us a signal when Mrs. Horvath had rounded the corner of the corridor. Then he closed our classroom door.

Wendy stood on her desk and announced, "The trial of Blubber will begin."

Linda was drawing a picture on vanilla paper. She looked up when Wendy said that.

"Did you hear me, Blubber? You're on trial!"

"I am not," Linda said.

Wendy laughed. "Oh yes you are. And I'm the judge."

"I don't want to play that game," Linda said.

"It's not a game," Wendy told her. "You're on trial for telling Mr. Machinist about Jill and Tracy on Halloween."

"I didn't tell anything."

"Don't lie, you smelly whale!" Wendy said. She got off her desk and stood close to Linda. She held up the picture Linda had been drawing, showed it to the rest of the class, then tore it in half.

Linda looked around at us, then she jumped up so fast that she knocked her chair over backwards. She ran for the door.

"Catch her," Wendy yelled. "Don't let her out of the room."

Robby and Irwin caught Linda and held on even though she was thrashing all around.

"Get the keys to the supply closet," Wendy told Caroline. "Quick . . ."

"Where?"

"Mrs. Minish's top drawer."

Caroline ran to Mrs. Minish's desk and fumbled around inside the top drawer. She held up a key. "Is this it?" she asked Wendy.

"Yes . . . throw . . . " Wendy caught the key and unlocked the supply closet. "Get her in here," she told the boys.

Robby and Irwin shoved Linda into the closet. Then they slammed the door and Wendy turned the key, leaving it in the lock.

"Let me out of here," Linda called. Her voice was muffled.

"Just shut up and listen to me, Blubber," Wendy said. "You're on trial for being a stool pigeon, a rat, a fink, and a tattletale. How do you plead . . . guilty or not guilty?"

"Let me out of here!" Linda shouted.

"Shut up!" Wendy told her. "How do you plead . . . guilty or not guilty?"

"Not guilty," Linda said. "Open the door . . . please!" She banged on it.

"Ladies and gentlemen of the jury," Wendy began, "it is your job to decide if Blubber is lying. Frankly, as the judge, I'm sure she is. We will hear the evidence from Jill Brenner, the class lawyer."

"Open the door," Linda called, just as I was about to begin giving evidence. "Open it or I'll scream!"

"You do and you're dead," Wendy said.

Linda quieted down.

"Hey . . . wait a second . . ." Rochelle said, and everybody turned to look at her because she never says anything. "Who's Blubber's lawyer?"

"Blubber's lawyer?" Wendy asked. "She doesn't get a lawyer."

"Oh yes she does," Rochelle said. "Every trial has two lawyers . . . one for the defense and one for the prosecution."

"Stay out of this, Rochelle," Wendy said.

I hit my head with my hand. "You know something . . . she's right. We did forget to give Blubber a lawyer."

"I want a lawyer!" Linda cried, banging on the door.

"I'm the judge here and I say we do it the way we planned."

"Look Wendy," I began, "my father's a lawyer and what Rochelle says is true. If we're going to do this we're going to do it right, otherwise it's not a real trial. And since the trial was *my* idea in the first place I say she gets a lawyer!"

"Are you done?" Wendy asked me.

I nodded.

"Good," she said, raising her voice. "Because you're ruining everything! You're turning chicken just like your chink friend."

"Don't you dare call Tracy a chink!"

"I'll call her whatever I damn please . . . and that's what she is."

I glared at Wendy. Then I turned around and said, "Rochelle . . . you want to be Blubber's lawyer?"

"I'm not sure," Rochelle said. "I'll have to think about it."

From inside the supply closet Linda called, "Rochelle . . . please be my lawyer."

"Okay," Rochelle said, "I guess I will. But

I'll need some time with my client to get the facts straight." She stood up.

"Stay right where you are, Rochelle!" Wendy said. "I'm running this trial." She looked at me. "And don't you forget it."

Rochelle waited to see what would happen next. And the rest of the class got very quiet. I thought about Tracy and how she said I'm scared of Wendy. And I thought about how worried I'd been on Monday, when Wendy got mad at me, and how good I'd felt when she wasn't mad anymore. And then I thought about Linda. Right that minute it didn't matter to me whether or not she had told on us. It was the trial that was important and it wasn't fair to have a trial without two lawyers. So I faced Wendy and I said, "I'm sick of you bossing everyone around. If Blubber doesn't get a lawyer then Blubber doesn't get a trial."

"No lawyer!" Wendy folded her arms across her chest.

"Then no trial!" I shouted, running to the supply closet. Before Wendy knew what I was doing I unlocked the door and flung it open.

"Come out! I just cancelled your trial."

"You'll pay for this," Wendy told me. "You'll be sorry you were ever born, Jill Brenner!"

For the first time I looked right into Wendy's eyes and I didn't like what I saw.

That afternoon Mrs. Minish said, "You've been such a nice, quiet class since lunch. I wish you'd act this way more often."

After school I went over to Tracy's. She was cleaning out the chicken coop. "Need any help?" I asked.

Tracy tossed me a broom and we swept together.

"I'm not hanging around with Wendy anymore," I told her. "She acts like she owns the whole world."

"I've always known that," Tracy said.

When the coop was clean Tracy picked up Friendly. "You want to hold him?" she asked.

"You know I do."

We sat down on the back steps. I held Friendly close and stroked his feathers. We were quiet for a while. Best friends don't have to talk all the time. Finally I said, "Tracy . . . do you think it was Linda who told on us?"

"I'm not sure . . . it could have been . . . if she was mad enough."

I nodded.

"Or it could have been Wendy and Caroline."

"Yeah . . . I guess you're right," I said. "It could have been."

"Or maybe even somebody else."

I thought about that. "Do you think we'll ever find out the truth?"

"Probably not."

Friendly flapped his wings and I let go of him. He ran after a chicken and tried to climb on her back. "He wants to mate," I said.

"Oh him . . ." Tracy laughed. "That's all he ever thinks about."

17

"What's with her?"

Mrs. Wu drove us to school the next morning because Tracy's project on the explorers was too big to carry on the bus. It barely fit into the car.

I was really glad I didn't have to take the bus because this way I wouldn't have to face Wendy first thing. It's hard not to be scared of her and the things she might do to me. I've made up my mind though. I will act the same as always except I'll just ignore Wendy. That will teach her a lesson about threatening people. She'll never make me feel sorry I was born.

When I walked into class Linda was sitting in my place. "Your desk is over there now," Wendy said, pointing to where Linda used to sit.

"Who gave you permission to move my desk, Blubber?" I asked, ignoring Wendy, just like I'd planned.

"Watch how you talk to *my* friend," Wendy said. "Her name is Linda and don't you forget it, B.B."

Everybody laughed. What did B.B. mean? And since when was Linda Wendy's friend?

Mrs. Minish came into the room. I went up to her. "Mrs. Minish . . . somebody moved my desk."

"Oh . . . the custodian is always moving desks around when he sweeps."

"Can I move it back where it belongs?"

Mrs. Minish looked around the classroom. "Why don't you move it next to Donna Davidson's . . . there's a space over there."

I went to my desk, stood the chair on top of it, and pushed it across the room, next to Donna's desk. When I did, she moved hers away and whispered, "Who wants to sit next to B.B."

When it was time for gym, Mr. Witneski

chose Bruce and Linda for the captains. Linda picked Wendy first. I waited and waited but nobody chose me for a team. When I was the only one left Linda told Bruce, "You get B.B." And all the kids on Bruce's team moaned.

I'll show them, I thought. I'll show them all. I will play so good I'll kick ten home runs.

But I didn't. I kicked three fly balls right to Wendy and each time I did my team said, "What can you expect from B.B.?"

At lunch I found out B.B. means Baby Brenner. It could have been worse. Wendy put a diaper pin on my desk with a note attached to it.

Baby Brenner better change her diapers.
She's smelling up the whole room!

After I read the note I said, "Ha ha . . ." remembering that my mother told me a person should always be able to laugh at herself. I tried to laugh as hard as the rest of the kids to show what a good sport I can be.

"Goo goo . . ." Robby Winters said. "See Baby Brenner laugh!" He sounded like he was reading from a first-grade book.

"See Baby Brenner eat!" Caroline said.

"Baby Brenner eats only mushy-gushy foods like peanut butter," Wendy told everyone, "because Baby Brenner can't chew big people's food yet."

I didn't finish my lunch.

That afternoon, when I got on the bus, Wendy stuck out her foot and tripped me. I fell flat on my face and my books flew all over the place. I tried to laugh again but this time the laugh just wouldn't come. Tracy helped me up, collected my books and led me to the seat she'd been saving.

"See Baby Brenner!" Wendy shouted. "Baby Brenner hasn't learned to walk yet."

The next day they all held their noses when I came near them. In the Girls' Room Donna Davidson shoved me against the sink and I got a black and blue mark on my leg. As I was getting a drink from the fountain, Caroline pushed me and I wound up with water all over my face.

During lunch period Wendy wrote on the blackboard, *B.B. loves W.W.*

"What's that mean?" Irwin asked.

"Baby Brenner is in love," Wendy said. "Baby Brenner is in love with Warren Winkler."

That was just too much. "I am not!" I told everybody. "That's a big lie!"

Then Wendy whispered something to Linda and both of them laughed.

On the playground we jumped rope. I knew I'd be last on line and I was. I bit my nails the whole time I was waiting.

"What's for dinner?" I asked Great Maudie, throwing my books down.

"Whatever your mother brings home," Great Maudie said. She was in one of her Yoga positions, with her legs crossed Indian style and her arms out straight.

"I wish you knew how to cook!" I ran for my room, bumping into Kenny on the way.

"Watch where you're going," he said.

"Shut up, carnivore!" I shouted at him.

I heard him ask Great Maudie, "What's with her?"

Great Maudie sighed and told him, "A bad day, I suppose."

I slammed my bedroom door and sat down at my desk.

Friday, November 22

Dear Mrs. Sandmeier,

I hope you're having fun in Switzerland. Nothing is very good at home. Do you believe that bad things always happen in threes? Grandma once told me that and I'm beginning to think it's true. Great Maudie turned out to be a terrible baby-sitter. She believes in cold showers, morning exercises, and crazy things to eat such as carrot juice and wheat germ mush. She can't cook regular foods at all. That is, she won't! So every night Mom and Dad bring our supper home from a take-out place. I am surviving on peanut butter. Did you know it's not bad with bananas?

I've been thinking that the next time you go on vacation and if it isn't the summer when me and Kenny are at camp, maybe we should ask Grandma to come after all. She's a good cook. She can make soup from real chicken. And besides, her hobby is cleaning. Mom already announced that we are going to spend all day tomorrow doing that.

Things are not the greatest in school either. I am having this special problem. It doesn't have to do with reading or math or anything like that. It's much worse. A lot of people don't like me anymore. And for no good reason. I'm trying hard to pretend it doesn't matter, but the truth is, it does. Sometimes I feel like crying but I hold it in. I wouldn't want to spoil your vacation so I won't say anything else.

I hope your mother is having a nice birthday and that you hurry home to us. Tu m'as beaucoup manqué.

Love,
Jill

Mom and Dad brought home Chinese food for supper. "What about me?" I said. "What am I supposed to eat?"

"Oh, Jill . . ." Mom said. "It's time you learned to eat like everyone else."

"Everyone else doesn't eat that stuff."

"What your mother means," Dad said, "is that practically everyone likes Chinese food. It's very popular in this country."

"Egg rolls and spare ribs and chow mein are not Chinese foods," I said. "If you don't believe me just ask Tracy . . . she'll tell you."

"Tracy's American," Kenny said.

"She's Chinese-American."

"She eats hot dogs."

"So?" I swallowed hard and nibbled on my nails.

"When did you start biting your nails again?" Mom asked.

I didn't answer her.

Dad said, "What about our deal? You haven't forgotten all those stamps at Gimbels, have you?"

I didn't answer him either.

When we sat down to supper I didn't feel like eating anything, not even the bread and cheese I knew Mom had put out just for me. My throat was tight and I had a pain in my stomach. "I'm not very hungry," I said.

"Are you getting sick?" Mom asked, touching my forehead.

"No . . ." I managed to say, before the tears came. I pushed my chair away from the table and ran for my room.

"You want to talk about it?" Mom asked, a few minutes later, as she sat on the edge of my bed.

"What?" I said, like I didn't know.

"Whatever's bothering you. It might make you feel better."

"Nobody likes me anymore," I told her. Then I started crying hard.

Mom held me. "I know . . . I know how it hurts."

"I hate them all . . ."

"Now . . . now . . ." Mom said, smoothing my hair.

"I do!"

"Maybe that's the trouble. You can be a pretty tough character sometimes . . ."

"Even so . . . it still isn't fair."

"Lots of things aren't fair."

"You told me a person who can laugh at herself will be respected."

"True."

"So I laughed," I said. "I tried to show I didn't care."

"That's good."

"But they don't respect me . . . they don't even like me . . . I need a tissue," I said, sniffling.

Mom handed one to me and I blew my nose.

"It's rough to be on the other side, isn't it?" she asked.

18

"Never mind spitting."

We spent all day Saturday cleaning the house, just like my mother promised. My job was dusting everything in sight. Dad scrubbed the bathrooms and kitchen while Mom changed the beds and went to the supermarket. Kenny got to vacuum. Great Maudie watered the plants.

I didn't start my math homework until Sunday night. I'm not supposed to wait till the last minute but somehow, I always do. It took me over an hour to finish and then I gave the paper to Dad to check. He said it was perfect. I was really pleased.

Talking to Mom on Friday night helped me

feel a little better about going back to school on Monday. But even so, I wasn't taking any chances. I wouldn't wear a skirt for anything.

Pants were much safer. That way Wendy couldn't force me to show the boys my underwear.

I called for Tracy and told her, "If they try to make me kiss Bruce I'll spit on them. That's what he said he'd do to Blubber if she touched his lips."

"Never mind spitting," Tracy said. "If they try anything at all you should bite them."

"I should?"

"Yes. I once read a news article about this woman who bit off another woman's finger. The human bite is very dangerous."

"I'll remember that," I said.

When we got to our bus stop a group of kids was coming over the hill, heading in our direction. When I saw who they were my heart started thumping. "What's going on?" I asked.

"I don't know," Tracy answered, "but we better find out."

Wendy, Caroline, Donna and Linda were first, with Robby, Michael and Irwin right behind them. They looked like an army.

"What're you doing here?" Tracy asked as they got to our corner. "You get the bus at Hidden Valley."

"Not today," Wendy said and she charged into me, knocking my things to the ground. Before I had a chance to pick everything up Wendy grabbed my math book and she and the others started playing catch with it.

"Cut that out!" I yelled, trying to get my book back. But they threw it over my head. I couldn't stop them from doing whatever they wanted.

"Give it to her!" Tracy hollered and she bopped Robby with her notebook.

Just as Irwin caught my book I kicked him as hard as I could, figuring he would drop it. But instead, he kicked me back and tossed my book into the street. I won't cry, I thought. I'll never let them see me cry. Never!

Our bus came along then, flashing its red stop lights. I ran into the street to get my math book, then Tracy helped me put my lunch back together because somebody had pulled it all apart. As I climbed onto the bus the driver yelled at me for taking too long. When I finally sat down next to Tracy I saw that Wendy and Linda were sharing a seat. Caroline sat alone, behind them.

Later, when Mrs. Minish collected our math homework, I couldn't find mine. "But I did it, Mrs. Minish," I said. "You can ask my father. He checked it for me."

"Maybe you left it at home." Mrs. Minish didn't seem to care.

I said, "No . . . I'm positive I put it inside my book."

"Maybe it fell out," Mrs. Minish told me.

"No!" I said, suddenly sure of what had happened to it. "It didn't *just* fall out!"

"Well, Jill . . . since this is the first time you've ever forgotten your homework I won't count it against you."

"But I didn't forget it," I said. "I told you I didn't forget it."

"All right, Jill. Don't worry about it. If you find it you can hand it in tomorrow."

"I'll do it over," I said.

"You can if you want to, but it really isn't necessary. Now . . . let's all take out our math books and open to Chapter Three."

Wendy turned around and smiled. I wanted to kill her.

When we went to the Girls' Room Wendy blocked the toilets and wouldn't let me use one until I said, *I am Baby Brenner. I'm not toilet trained yet. That's why I stink.*

I shook my head at her.

"You have to say it!" Wendy told me.

"No way," I said. "I won't."

"Then I'll have to check your diapers myself."

I thought about making a run for it, but Wendy had Caroline, Donna and Linda on her side and I wasn't sure I had anyone on mine. So I said, "You touch me and you're dead!"

"Grab her, Caroline!" Wendy said. "Grab her arms and I'll pull her smelly diapers off."

Caroline is bigger than me and stronger too. As she came toward me I shouted, "You always do what Wendy says? Don't you have a mind of your own?"

"I have a mind of my own."

"Then why don't you use it for once! Wendy doesn't even like you anymore so why should you follow her orders?"

"Shut up, Brenner!" Wendy said. "Don't listen to her, Caroline."

"She does too like me," Caroline said.

"Then how come she's always hanging around Linda? Didn't you see them this morning, on the bus? I'll bet she's not even your partner for the class trip."

Caroline looked at Wendy. "We're partners, aren't we?"

Before Wendy could answer, Linda said, "I'm Wendy's partner." She hung an arm over Wendy's shoulder.

Caroline bit her lip, turned and walked out of the Girls' Room. Donna followed her.

"Don't you ever answer for me again!" Wendy told Linda.

Linda looked as if Wendy had slapped her in the face.

I didn't wait around to see what Wendy would do next. I opened the door to a toilet and locked myself in the booth. I was really shaking. Before I came out I checked underneath to make sure there were no feet in sight. That way I knew I was safe.

Nobody called me Baby Brenner during lunch. Donna and Caroline moved their desks together and Wendy invited Laurie to eat with her. Linda sat alone at her desk, the way she used to.

I took out my sandwich and looked at it, thinking how much better it would taste if I had someone to talk to. I hate to eat all by myself. I glanced around the room, wondering, should I or shouldn't I? Oh, I might as well try, I finally decided. You sometimes have to make the first move or else you might wind up like Linda—letting other people decide what's going to happen to you.

I stood up, walked over to Rochelle's desk and said, "Hey Rochelle . . . you want to eat with me?"

Rochelle didn't answer right away and for a second I was sorry I'd asked her. But then she finished chewing, swallowed whatever was in her mouth, and said, "Why not?"

I moved my desk next to hers. She had a peanut butter sandwich too.

19

"Put your money where your mouth is."

Tuesday morning, on the way to school, Irwin called me some of his best names. I said, "The same to you," and everybody laughed, but not at me.

That afternoon we had our Thanksgiving program. The sixth graders put on a boring play about the Pilgrims, the Indians and the first Thanksgiving. I wish our school could do a play like the one in *Harriet the Spy* where everybody pretends to be a different vegetable. I would like to play the onion. I'd roll around the floor the way Harriet did in the book. I wonder if there really are schools where they do that kind of thing?

When we got back to class Mrs. Minish stayed out in the hall, talking to the teacher from the next room. So Robby Winters had plenty of time to stick pins through his fingers and do his zombie act. When he shoved his hands in my face I said, "What's so great about that? Anybody can do it."

"Oh yeah . . ."

"Yeah . . ."

"Including you?"

"Including me."

"Put your money where your mouth is, Brenner."

"How much?" I asked him.

"A quarter."

"You're on . . . give me some pins."

Robby took the pins out of his fingers and handed them to me. I stuck one through the top layer of skin of every finger, being careful not to flinch as I did. Then I stood up, held my hands out straight, and walked around making zombie noises.

"Exactly what is going on here?" Mrs. Minish stood in the doorway, watching me.

"Jill . . . you're out of your seat."

"Yes, Mrs. Minish." I hurried back to my desk, hid my hands underneath it and pulled the pins out of my fingers.

Robby passed me a quarter.

By lunchtime it was easy to tell that Wendy and Laurie were going to be best friends and so were Donna and Caroline. Some people are *always* changing best friends. I'm glad me and Tracy aren't that way. Still, it's nice to have a regular friend in your class, even if it's not a *best* friend. I ate lunch with Rochelle again. She's kind of quiet but I get the feeling that a lot goes on inside her head. So later, when it was time to go home, and we all ran for our lockers, I said, "Hey Rochelle . . . you want to be my partner for the class trip?"

She put on her jacket, closed her locker door, and said, "Why not?"

I didn't bite my nails once that afternoon or night and when Dad tucked me into bed I said, "You know something? There's still a whole month to go before Christmas."

"So?" he asked.

"So . . . is our deal still on?" I held out my hands and wiggled my fingers to show him what I was talking about.

"It's still on," he told me.

"Good . . . because I think I can make it this time."

We had just half a day of school on Wednesday. On the bus ride home we played Keep-Away with Robby's hat and the sixth graders taught us a song about the girls in France. The bus driver yelled, "Shut up or I'll report you to the principal."

Nobody paid any attention.

When we got off the bus me and Tracy stopped for the mail. Both of us had a packet of approvals from Winthrop.

"Come over and we'll decide what to buy," I said.

"As soon as I change."

"Don't forget your album."

"How could I?" Tracy asked.

Kenny met me at the front door. "Did

you know the longest earthworm in the world measures twenty-one feet when fully extended?"

"I'm really glad to hear that," I said. "His mother must be very proud."

Judy Blume talks about writing *Blubber*

When my daughter was in fifth grade the class leader used her power in an evil way to turn everyone in the class against one girl. This bully (like Wendy in the book) made the other girl's life miserable. My daughter was the shy, quiet girl in the class, the observer, like Rochelle. She was upset by what was going on, but she didn't know what to do about it. I think she was scared. Like many other kids in that class, she worried she could wind up the next victim of the bully.

I wrote *Blubber* because bullying is often kept a secret by the kids who see it happening, and even by the person who's being bullied. Being bullied feels so humiliating, it's such a terrible and frightening experience, that kids are often afraid to tell anyone, even their parents. But keeping it a secret doesn't help anyone. It just makes it worse. It leaves the bully thinking she or he can get away with anything. I hope this story will help kids, parents, and teachers to start talking and working together. No more secrets. If it happens to you, talk to the people you trust most. It's too hard to worry alone.

Can't get enough Judy Blume?

Turn the page to start reading
Are You There God? It's Me, Margaret.,
Judy Blume's unforgettable story about
choosing a religion, buying a bra,
and everything in between.

Are you there God? It's me, Margaret.
We're moving today. I'm so scared
God. I've never lived anywhere but
here. Suppose I hate my new school?
Suppose everybody there hates me?
Please help me God. Don't let New
Jersey be too horrible. Thank you.

We moved on the Tuesday before Labor Day. I knew
what the weather was like the second I got up. I knew
because I caught my mother sniffing under her arms.
She always does that when it's hot and humid, to
make sure her deodorant's working. I don't use
deodorant yet. I don't think people start to smell bad
until they're at least twelve. So I've still got a few
months to go.

I was really surprised when I came home from

camp and found out our New York apartment had been rented to another family and that *we* owned a house in Farbrook, New Jersey. First of all I never even heard of Farbrook. And second of all, I'm not usually left out of important family decisions.

But when I groaned, "Why New Jersey?" I was told, "Long Island is too social—Westchester is too expensive—and Connecticut is too inconvenient."

So Farbrook, New Jersey it was, where my father could commute to his job in Manhattan, where I could go to public school, and where my mother could have all the grass, trees and flowers she ever wanted. Except I never knew she wanted that stuff in the first place.

The new house is on Morningbird Lane. It isn't bad. It's part brick, part wood. The shutters and front door are painted black. Also, there is a very nice brass knocker. Every house on our new street looks a lot the same. They are all seven years old. So are the trees.

I think we left the city because of my grandmother, Sylvia Simon. I can't figure out any other reason for the move. Especially since my mother says Grandma is too much of an influence on me. It's no big secret in our family that Grandma sends me to summer camp in New Hampshire. And that she enjoys paying my private school tuition (which she won't be able to do any more because now I'll be going to public school). She even knits me sweaters that have labels sewed inside saying MADE EXPRESSLY FOR YOU . . . BY GRANDMA.

And she doesn't do all that because we're poor. I know for a fact that we're not. I mean, we aren't rich but we certainly have enough. Especially since I'm an only child. That cuts way down on food and clothes. I know this family that has seven kids and every time they go to the shoe store it costs a bundle. My mother and father didn't plan for me to be an only child, but that's the way it worked out, which is fine with me because this way I don't have anybody around to fight.

Anyhow, I figure this house-in-New-Jersey business is my parents' way of getting me away from Grandma. She doesn't have a car, she hates buses *and* she thinks all trains are dirty. So unless Grandma plans to walk, which is unlikely, I won't be seeing much of her. Now some kids might think, who cares about seeing a grandmother? But Sylvia Simon is a lot of fun, considering her age, which I happen to know is sixty. The only problem is she's always asking me if I have boyfriends and if they're Jewish. Now *that* is ridiculous because number one I don't have boyfriends. And number two what would I care if they're Jewish or not?

We hadn't been in the new house more than an hour when the doorbell rang. I answered. It was this girl in a bathing suit.

"Hi," she said. "I'm Nancy Wheeler. The real estate agent sent out a sheet on you. So I know you're Margaret and you're in sixth grade. So am I."

I wondered what else she knew.

"It's plenty hot, isn't it?" Nancy asked.

"Yes," I agreed. She was taller than me and had bouncy hair. The kind I'm hoping to grow. Her nose turned up so much I could look right into her nostrils.

Nancy leaned against the door. "Well, you want to come over and go under the sprinklers?"

"I don't know. I'll have to ask."

"Okay. I'll wait."

I found my mother with her rear end sticking out

of a bottom kitchen cabinet. She was arranging her pots and pans.

"Hey Mom. There's a girl here who wants to know if I can go under her sprinklers?"

"If you want to," my mother said.

"I need my bathing suit," I said.

"Gads, Margaret! I don't know where a bathing suit is in this mess."

I walked back to the front door and told Nancy, "I can't find my bathing suit."

"You can borrow one of mine," she said.

"Wait a second," I said, running back to the kitchen. "Hey Mom. She says I can wear one of hers. Okay?"

"Okay," my mother mumbled from inside the cabinet. Then she backed out. She spit her hair out of her face. "What did you say her name was?"

"Umm . . . Wheeler. Nancy Wheeler."

"Okay. Have a good time," my mother said.

Nancy lives six houses away, also on Morningbird Lane. Her house looks like mine but the brick is painted white and the front door and shutters are red.

"Come on in," Nancy said.

I followed her into the foyer, then up the four stairs leading to the bedrooms. The first thing I noticed about Nancy's room was the dressing table with the heartshaped mirror over it. Also, everything was very neat.

When I was little I wanted a dressing table like that. The kind that's wrapped up in a fluffy organdy skirt. I never got one though, because my mother likes tailored things.

Nancy opened her bottom dresser drawer. "When's your birthday?" she asked.

"March," I told her.

"Great! We'll be in the same class. There are three sixth grades and they arrange us by age. I'm April."

"Well, I don't know what class I'm in but I know it's Room Eighteen. They sent me a lot of forms to fill out last week and that was printed on all of them."

"I told you we'd be together. I'm in Room Eighteen too." Nancy handed me a yellow bathing suit. "It's clean," she said. "My mother always washes them after a wearing."

"Thank you," I said, taking the suit. "Where should I change?"

Nancy looked around the room. "What's wrong with here?"

"Nothing," I said. "I don't mind if you don't mind."

"Why should I mind?"

"I don't know." I worked the suit on from the bottom. I knew it was going to be too big. Nancy gave me the creeps the way she sat on her bed and watched me. I left my polo on until the last possible second. I wasn't about to let her see I wasn't growing yet. That was my business.

"Oh, you're still flat." Nancy laughed.

"Not exactly," I said, pretending to be very cool. "I'm small boned, is all."

"I'm growing already," Nancy said, sticking her chest way out. "In a few years I'm going to look like one of those girls in *Playboy*."

Well, I didn't think so, but I didn't say anything. My father gets *Playboy* and I've seen those girls in the middle. Nancy looked like she had a long way to go. Almost as far as me.

"Want me to do up your straps?" she asked.

"Okay."

"I figured you'd be real grown up coming from New York. City girls are supposed to grow up a lot faster. Did you ever kiss a boy?"

"You mean really kiss? On the lips?" I asked.

"Yes," Nancy said impatiently. "Did you?"

"Not really," I admitted.

Nancy breathed a sigh of relief. "Neither did I."

I was overjoyed. Before she said that I was beginning to feel like some kind of underdeveloped little kid.

"I practice a lot though," Nancy said.

"Practice what?" I asked.

"Kissing! Isn't that what we were talking about? *Kissing*!"

"How can you practice that?" I asked.

"Watch this." Nancy grabbed her bed pillow and embraced it. She gave it a long kiss. When she was done she threw the pillow back on the bed. "It's important to experiment, so when the time comes you're all ready. I'm going to be a great kisser some day. Want to see something else?"

I just stood there with my mouth half open. Nancy sat down at her dressing table and opened a drawer. "Look at this," she said.

I looked. There were a million little bottles, jars and tubes. There were more cosmetics in that drawer than my mother had all together. I asked, "What do you do with all that stuff?"

"It's another one of my experiments. To see how I look best. So when the time comes I'll be ready." She opened a lipstick and painted on a bright pink mouth. "Well, what do you think?"

"Umm . . . I don't know. It's kind of bright, isn't it?"

Nancy studied herself in the heartshaped mirror. She rubbed her lips together. "Well, maybe you're right." She wiped off the lipstick with a tissue. "My mother would kill me if I came out like this anyway. I can't wait till eighth grade. That's when I'll be allowed to wear lipstick every day."

Then she whipped out a hairbrush and started to brush her long, brown hair. She parted it in the middle and caught it at the back with a barrette. "Do you always wear your hair like that?" she asked me.

My hand went up to the back of my neck. I felt all the bobby pins I'd used to pin my hair up so my neck wouldn't sweat. I knew it looked terrible. "I'm letting it grow," I said. "It's at that in-between stage now. My mother thinks I should wear it over my ears though. My ears stick out a little."

"I noticed," Nancy said.

I got the feeling that Nancy noticed *everything*!

"Ready to go?" she asked.

"Sure."

She opened a linen closet in the hall and handed me a purple towel. I followed her down the stairs and into the kitchen, where she grabbed two peaches out of the refrigerator and handed one to me. "Want to meet my mom?" she asked.

"Okay," I said, taking a bite of my peach.

"She's thirty-eight, but tells us she's twenty-five. Isn't that a scream!" Nancy snorted.

Mrs. Wheeler was on the porch with her legs tucked under her and a book on her lap. I couldn't tell what book it was. She was suntanned and had the same nose as Nancy.

"Mom, this is Margaret Simon who just moved in down the street."

Mrs. Wheeler took off her glasses and smiled at me.

"Hello," I said.

"Hello, Margaret. I'm very glad to meet you. You're from New York, aren't you?"

"Yes, I am."

"East side or West?"

"We lived on West Sixty-seventh. Near Lincoln Center."

"How nice. Does your father still work in the city?"

"Yes."

"And what does he do?"

"He's in insurance." I sounded like a computer.

"How nice. Please tell your mother I'm looking forward to meeting her. We've got a Morningbird

Lane bowling team on Mondays and a bridge game every other Thursday afternoon and a . . ."

"Oh, I don't think my mother knows how to bowl and she wouldn't be interested in bridge. She paints most of the day," I explained.

"She paints?" Mrs. Wheeler asked.

"Yes."

"How interesting. What does she paint?"

"Mostly pictures of fruits and vegetables. Sometimes flowers too."

Mrs. Wheeler laughed. "Oh, you mean *pictures*! I thought you meant walls! Tell your mother we're making our car pools early this year. We'd be happy to help her arrange hers . . . especially Sunday school. That's always the biggest problem."

"I don't go to Sunday school."

"You don't?"

"No."

"*Lucky!*" Nancy shouted.

"Nancy, *please!*" Mrs. Wheeler said.

"Hey Mom . . . Margaret came to go under the sprinkler with me, not to go through the third degree."

"All right. If you see Evan tell him I want to talk to him."

Nancy grabbed me by the hand and pulled me outside. "I'm sorry my mother's so nosey."

"I didn't mind," I said. "Who's Evan?"

"He's my brother. He's disgusting!"

"Disgusting how?" I asked.

"Because he's fourteen. All boys of fourteen are disgusting. They're only interested in two things—pictures of naked girls and dirty books!"

Nancy really seemed to know a lot. Since I didn't know any boys of fourteen I took her word for it.

Nancy turned on the outside faucet and adjusted it so that the water sprayed lightly from the sprinkler. "Follow the leader!" she called, running through the water. I guessed Nancy was the leader.

She jumped through the spray. I followed. She turned cartwheels. I tried but didn't make it. She did leaps through the air. I did too. She stood straight under the spray. I did the same. That's when the water came on full blast. We both got drenched, including our hair.

"Evan, you stinker!" Nancy shrieked. "I'm telling!" She ran off to the house and left me alone with two boys.

"Who're you?" Evan asked.

"I'm Margaret. We just moved in."

"Oh. This is Moose," he said, pointing to the other boy.

I nodded.

"Hey," Moose said. "If you just moved in, ask your father if he's interested in having me cut his lawn. Five bucks a week and I trim too. What'd you say your last name was?"

"I didn't. But it's Simon." I couldn't help thinking about what Nancy said—that all they were interested in was dirty books and naked girls. I held my towel tight around me in case they were trying to sneak a look down my bathing suit.

"Evan! Come in here this instant!" Mrs. Wheeler hollered from the porch.

"I'm coming . . . I'm coming," Evan muttered.

After Evan went inside Moose said, "Don't forget to tell your father. *Moose Freed.* I'm in the phone book."

"I won't forget," I promised.

Moose nibbled a piece of grass. Then the back door slammed and Nancy came out, red-eyed and sniffling.

"Hey, Nancy baby! Can't you take a joke?" Moose asked.

ALL OF THE QUESTIONS.
ALL OF THE ANSWERS.

Judy Blume has a whole new look!
Which one will you read first?